TANIA WEATHERLEY

Y2K Betrayal

First published by Tania Weatherley Books 2025

Cover design by GetCovers

www.taniaweatherley.com

tania.weatherly.author@gmail.com

First edition

ISBN: 978-1-7641381-4-7

This book was professionally typeset on Reedsy.
Find out more at reedsy.com

A Dash of Downunder

This book is written in British English, sprinkled with plenty of Australian phrases to keep things interesting! So, you might notice an 's' where you'd expect a 'z' or see 'chips' instead of 'fries'. There are probably more quirks, but you get the gist.

If you need any clarification, check out my Aussie slang glossary.

Content Warning

This story delves into mature themes, including complex relationships involving emotional manipulation and infidelity, heavy substance use (alcohol), and moments of physical violence and assault. It also explores deep emotional trauma stemming from parental abandonment and unresolved grief, leading to challenges related to self-worth, control issues, and deep emotional voids. While the narrative contains elements of romance, certain explicit or emotionally charged passages may be intense or distressing for some readers. Please take care while reading, and remember that individual responses to sensitive material may vary.

Y2K Betrayal Playlist

Listen to the Full Playlist on Spotify

*The songs below are included throughout the story in **bold**.*

"Shine" by Vanessa Amorosi
"Lucky Me" by Bachelor Girl
"Genie in a Bottle" by Christina Aguilera
"Too Much" by The Spice Girls
"No Scrubs" by TLC
"Beautiful Stranger" by Madonna
"Need You Tonight" by INXS
"Tellin' Everybody" by Human Nature
"Say My Name" by Destiny's Child
"Breathe" by Kylie Minogue
"Pony" by Ginuwine
"Most Girls" by Pink
"I Want it That Way" by Backstreet Boys
"Steal My Sunshine" by LEN
"Boom, Boom, Boom, Boom" by the Vengaboys

"Every Morning" by Suger Ray

"Lovefool" by The Cardigans

"Smooth" By Santana and Rob Thomas

"Don't Call Me Baby" by Madison Avenue

"Man of The Hour" by John Farnham

"If You Could Read My Mind" by Ultra Nate, Amber & Jocelyn Enriquez

"Break Me, Shake Me" by Savage Garden

"Heartbeaker" by Mariah Carey

"Everywhere You Go" by Taxiride

"If You Had My Love" by Jennifer Lopez

"Linger" by the Cranberries

"Gotta Tell You" by Samantha Mumba

"Better Off Alone" by Alice Deejay

"Left Outside Alone" by Anastacia

"Why Does it Always Rain on Me" by Travis

"Bitch" by Meredith Brooks

"White Noise" by the Living End

"Shimmer" by Fuel

"(Simply) The Best" by Jimmy Barnes and Tina Turner

"Tip of My Tongue" by Diesel

"It Feels So Good" by Sonique

"Say You'll Be There" by The Spice Girls

"Kiss From a Rose" by Seal

"Not a Day Goes By" by Rick Price

"Closing Time" by Semisonic

"Groovejet (If This Aint Love)" by Spiller & Sophie Ellis Bextor

"Amazing" by Alex Lloyd

"You're Still the One" by Shania Twain

Prologue

Ah, the year 2000. A time when the nights were loud, the drinks were cheap, and the glitter never quite washed off. Clubbing was a ritual, not a hobby—an escape hatch from reality, where the bass drowned out your thoughts and the strobe lights made everyone look like they were living their best life. Or at least pretending to.

Fashion was chaotic in the best and worst ways. Mesh tops, vinyl pants, and sunglasses worn indoors. Boys in oversized jeans and frosted tips. Girls in halter necks and body glitter, dancing like their hearts depended on it. And maybe they did. Because beneath the sequins and sweat, something darker was brewing—a hunger for validation, a desperation to be seen, even if it was just through the lens of a disposable camera.

Alcohol flowed like water. Vodka Cruisers, Bacardi Breezers, and whatever neon-coloured cocktail the bartender could whip up. It wasn't about taste—it was about forgetting. Forgetting the week, the heartbreak, the gnawing sense that something was missing. Everyone was chasing a high, whether it came from a drink, a kiss, or a stranger's attention.

And then there were the mobile phones. The new and growing communication fad that would change the world.

Suddenly, it wasn't just about who you were with—it was about who was texting. Who had your number. Who was waiting on the other end of a glowing screen. Mobile phones weren't just gadgets—they were lifelines. Status symbols. Emotional crutches. The Nokia 3310 became a trophy, and texting turned into a new kind of intimacy. A new kind of betrayal.

The club scene shifted. Eyes flicked down mid-conversation. Messages were sent from bathroom stalls and dance floors. Relationships began and ended with a beep. The digital age wasn't just creeping in—it was crashing through the door, changing everything.

And David was right in the thick of it.

"Happy Birthday, my boy."

A mobile phone?

Another expensive gift to make up for what they lost.

David knew it. His dad knew it. They both accepted that fact of their relationship, and David milked it for all it was worth. Because it hurt. He hurt. And he liked to think all this *stuff* had a way to muffle it. Keep it covered.

His dad obviously hoped it would too. But David knew deep down it couldn't. So, he continued to take. And take. And take some more. In the hopes that one day, he'd take enough to feel full again.

Feel loved again.

Feel wanted again.

Chapter 1

Monique

"Here we go," Monique muttered, bracing herself. "'Would you consider yourself to be underweight, average weight, overweight, or obese?'"

"What kind of question is that?" the woman on the other end of the phone snapped. "This is ridiculous. You said this survey would take ten minutes. I've been stuck on the phone for twenty. I'm done."

Click. The engaged signal rang out.

"Argh," Monique groaned. So close—just two questions left.

She hated that damn survey question from one of their weight loss supplement clients.

Hell, she hated the whole call centre job.

And she felt sorry for the poor colleague who'd get stuck calling that number next.

If only people knew they had to ask not to be called again—hanging up didn't cut it.

That number just gets filtered back into the system, over and over, until someone either gives up and answers the whole survey... or learns the insider trick to request removal from the call list.

She clicked through the DOS screens to queue up the next call, but before she could connect, a bell rang out across the office. The team had hit their quota. Finally. Time to clock off.

Before she had a chance to get up, two hands landed on her shoulders from behind "Did you hear? Crazy Kathy's getting the boot!" Monique looked back to see Julie's too-wide smile beaming down at her.

"What? Why?" Monique blinked. Could Kathy really be gone? Their call centre team leader always came to work dressed like she had put her clothes on in the dark and barked out orders like a dictator.

"Janice caught her smoking dope at her desk after hours. That was it. Gone. They're announcing it tomorrow and looking to replace her ASAP."

So that's why Janice had been pacing the office like a stressed-out cockatoo.

"So you're telling me... her job's up for grabs?"

"Sure is," Julie said, eyes sparkling.

Monique's pulse quickened. This was an opportunity she couldn't ignore. She had dreams to chase—and a pay rise would get her one step closer.

She needed to get out of this city. Badly. Her dream of travelling the world was shackled by a pathetic savings account, but a bump in income could change that. Even if it meant more responsibility in a soul-sucking job surrounded by colleagues who thought she was a cold-faced bitch.

With her wavy red-wine hair pulled back, a button-up blouse, modest pencil skirt and no makeup, she was a corporate cardboard cutout. Unassuming. Un-remarkable. Just another headset-wearing drone reading scripted questions off a screen. Feeding retail giants data to help them sell more brand-name crap to unsuspecting consumers.

But it paid the bills. And more importantly, it gave her time to do what she truly loved: sing.

Once or twice a week, Monique stood in Brisbane's Queen Street Mall and sang. At first, she worried someone from work might recognise her. But no one ever did. Besides, she looked completely different when she performed—dressed to the nines, radiating sensuality, singing ballads that seeped into her soul. Songs that felt like they'd chosen her.

She didn't sing for money. She sang for the feeling. For the way strangers stopped and saw her—really saw her. That electric shiver of connection always left her craving more.

After three months of street performances, Samuel Sparks approached her one brisk winter night while singing **"Shine" by Vanessa Amorossi.**

"You're good," he said, handing her a business card for the Cyder Lounge. "Come sing at my joint. I'll give you a shot—but you've gotta turn up the heat. Your look. Your songs. I need talent that turns heads. You've got potential. And we've got a grand piano, so if you know someone who can play, even better."

Now, that dream of performing in front of a crowd—and getting paid for it—was about to become reality.

The weight of expectation she'd placed on herself tonight threatened to derail the performance she had to nail.

To calm her nerves, Monique sat at her gold vanity table, **"Lucky Me" by Bachelor Girl** playing softly in the background. Scissors in hand, she eyed the stack of *Cleo*, *Smash Hits*, and *Woman's Day* magazines waiting to be rifled through.

Skimming the pages of *Woman's Day*, its cover graced by Princess Diana, she paused—scissors poised mid-air.

She snipped out an image of a woman lounging in a beach chair, cocktail in hand—a promo for a summer fragrance. She rounded the edges, then glued it to her ever-growing collage: her vision board. A rim of glitter glue added extra sparkle.

On the left of her vision board masterpiece, she collected cutouts of beaches, landmarks and smiling travellers. On the right, Kyle Minogue, Mariah Carey, Shania Twain, Christina Aguilera, microphones, stages and adoring crowds. And in the centre, cut-out letters spelled: Fake it Till You Make it.

Every piece of perfectly trimmed paper represented little fragments of a life and dream she was determined to build. If she worked hard enough. Saved long enough. Kept her eye on the goal. She'd get there. She *would* get there. She had to. Because her heart and mind would never be satisfied living this mundane life. A life she didn't choose. She just fell into this shit heap, and it was crushing her soul.

Her mother wouldn't have approved. She'd wanted more for her. So much more.

If only she could see her now.

This was it. Tonight was her chance to snatch one of those dreams with both hands and hold on tight.

It was time to wear a new mask. A new costume.

One that screamed Jessica Rabbit. Sex on legs. Unapologetic vixen.

Did she feel self-conscious in all this makeup, heels, and barely-there clothing? Hell yes. But would she let anyone see that?

No way.

She'd play the role. Ooze confidence, seduction, and sex appeal.

And just like her vision board immortalised,

fake it till you make it, baby.

Chapter 2

David

A cute brunette walked up to the bar; her brown eyes glistened under her long lashes "Appletini, please."

David grabbed the liquor bottles and poured at speed, concocting the cocktail without breaking eye contact. His gaze never wavered from hers. He felt woozy. That shot he took before his shift was kicking in. But he steadied himself and poured out her beverage with perfect grace.

Just as she slid her hand over, wrapping her red nails around the glass rim, fingertips brushing his, he gently pulled the glass away from her grip, a cute wrinkle of confusion creasing her brow.

"Hold on, beautiful, I have something for you." David grabbed a white paper napkin and pen from his pocket, wrote down his number and slid it across the table alongside her beverage.

With a sly wink and smile, he added, "And the drink is on me. You're welcome."

She looked back over her shoulder toward the balding middle-aged dude in a suit, red-faced and laughing with a pack of matching suits. He knew she walked in here with him, hand in hand, but that didn't stop him from shooting his shot. She was too good-looking to be with that loser. Another ugly man pulling a beautiful young thing purely for his money. But was she satisfied with him? Really? David doubted it.

When the brunette turned back to face him, as expected, she snatched his number away into her handbag, pink flushing her cheeks and teeth tucked over her bottom lip as she drank him in with her eyes one last time before clasping her cocktail and meandered over to her date.

"You did not just give that girl a free drink." David turned his head to find his father, Samuel Sparks, behind him, scowling.

"What of it?" David scoffed as he headed to the back room, trying to create some distance from his father and failing miserably as his dad followed close behind.

"I am running a professional establishment here, son, and if other patrons see you giving away drinks, it's not a good look."

"Did you see her dad? Come on, like you wouldn't have offered her a drink for a shot with her?"

He didn't understand why his dad was being so hard on him. As soon as David was a legal adult, he practically pushed him to 'make the most of his youth.' And 'get some while he was young.' And he did. He had been living life like a legend for four years now, and he never wanted it to end, but over the last year or so, his dad's tone surrounding his lifestyle had soured significantly.

David put his arm up to lean against the door frame and missed, stumbling over his feet before righting himself.

"And you're drinking on the job too."

"Since when has that been a problem?"

His father sucked in a long, shaky breath before letting out an 'I don't know what to do with you' sigh.

Shaking his head with a look of disappointment and perhaps a touch of sadness and defeat in his eyes, he said, "It's...fine, son. Your shift's done. Go and find a spot to 'chill out' or whatever it is you young blokes say these days."

The silence that followed was thick—like the air before a summer storm, heavy with things unsaid.

He didn't meet his father's eyes, but he could feel the judgment radiating off him in waves.

His father's voice, when it came again, was clipped. Professional. Like flicking a switch from personal to business.

"I've got a new singer performing soon, but I'll be looking after guests in the VIP room when she sings. This singer is getting a trial run tonight. So, sit down, sober up and let me know if you think this one is worth keeping around."

David couldn't hold in his eye roll and sigh. He didn't want to sober up. He'd much rather round up the boys and take full advantage of the night ahead rather than being on talent scout duties. But that disappointed look in his dad's eyes stirred something inside him. He didn't like that look being pointed at him, so he would do this favour for his old man, because he gave a shit about what his dad thought about him, and he couldn't deny that deep down, he wanted to impress him, despite all of the evidence over the past few years proving otherwise. But he couldn't help it.

Doing the wrong thing, things other people couldn't get away with, gave him a thrill like nothing else. The feeling was addictive, and he craved it. The only time it was ever at least partially tethered was for the good of his old man, because he had already been through so much. They both had.

Samuel Sparks poured David a glass of water, handed it to him and pointed him towards the stage. As David made his way back through the bar and out towards the crowd of dignified drinkers, he looked back to check if his father was gone before pouring out the water in the nearby bar sink and filling it with vodka instead, right in eye shot of Kyle. His housemate and old friend from his high school days, who also happened to pick up shifts as a bartender at the Cyder Lounge. He shook his head and continued serving patrons. Good. He didn't need to get shit from him, too.

David had pretty low expectations for this so-called performer. The Cyder Lounge—the ritziest establishment on the strip, attracting only the wealthiest and most exclusive patrons—had a reputation to uphold. His father had a reputation to uphold, and whoever performed centre stage had to fit the mould too.

He was surprised his father was willing to take such a professional and personal risk by taking on a performer. If he or she did not live up to the high expectations of their patrons, it would not be a good look, and at worst, it could drive away guests and give their establishment a bad name.

They had only tried one performer before – a jazz pianist who deviated from favoured jazz tunes into his own alternative musical creations that simply did not gel with the crowd. He lasted all of a month before getting kicked to the curb, and instead opted for safer and far cheaper ambient music in the background while patrons drank and conversed. Whoever this was, David wouldn't let the embarrassment his father went through over that incident happen again. One wrong note and they would be out of there, no question.

A man stepped out onto the stage in a suit and tie with a gruff face and dishevelled hair and sat at the piano.

Oh great, another pianist. He did not want to give this bloke an ounce of his time or attention already, and he hadn't even started playing yet. David allowed his eyes to roam the room as he leaned against a wall in the corner between the stage and the bar, trying his best to spot the most beautiful prospects. His eyes zoned in on the brunette he had given his number to earlier.

And then, that voice. It broke through his consciousness like rippling waves of pleasure and intoxication.

The sound of that voice made him want to close his eyes and sink deeper into it.

That voice was sensual, intoxicating, alluring. The sum of all his desires bundled up and transformed into silky, soulful sounds.

Once his mind got over the pure euphoria of that voice, he recognised the words as **"Genie in a Bottle" by Christina Aguilera**. An even slower and more sultry but somehow still classy version of the original song. A better version when paired with that voice. As he finally turned to see the source of that incredible sound, his mouth nearly dropped to the floor at the sight of her.

A rich red leopard print dress traced her silhouette, the deep-red faux-fur shawl softening the edges. Thick, red-wine waves framed her face, matching her plump lips; frameless brown shades with a diamante heart at the corner finished the look, sprinkling her aura with an extra layer of effortless star power.

She was more than beautiful.

She was the sexiest damn woman he'd ever seen in his life, hands down, and that voice was an extra delicious cherry on top. He could hardly believe his eyes and ears, and the overwhelming feeling of shock, desire and unadulterated lust coursing through his veins was like nothing he'd ever felt before, and he didn't want that feeling to go away. It was too good.

She was going to be his.

He had to have her.

He would make sure of it.

The insatiable need swelling inside him was as persistent as if he were dying of thirst in the desert. She was that vital to his existence.

When the song ended, applause surrounded him. He even heard a wolf whistle amongst the crowd. He was so wrong. So very wrong. But he was glad he was.

Chapter 3

Monique

Monique held her breath in tight. She thought he sounded good. Did she really though, or was it all in her head? The silent seconds that passed felt like minutes until finally...applause and even a few wolf whistles radiated through the room—exactly the hit of validation she needed to breathe again. Despite wearing a mask of cool confidence for the crowd, her fingers trembled slightly as she clutched the microphone for dear life.

Her first round of applause. Real applause. For her. If a few gawkers and half-arsed claps from passers-by in the street lit a thrill within her, this crowd of 50 or so soaking her in felt like a full-blown bonfire of euphoria, and she did not want that flame to die out.

This was a dream come true. No doubt about it. As her face split into a million-watt smile that would've put Times Square to shame, Monique had one crystal-clear thought: this feeling? Better than Tim Tams, better than Christmas morning, better than... well, almost everything. But this was only the beginning. She had a whole night's worth of songs left to go, and she couldn't be more thrilled about it. Time to suck them in and keep them coming back for more.

"Good evening, darlings... I'm Monique Chambers, and I'll be weaving a little musical magic for you tonight. The champagne may be chilled, but I promise to keep things... warm. So loosen those ties, sink into those leather chairs, and let me paint your evening in shades of velvet and jazz."

As she began to sing the next song in her set, she noticed him. He stood in the shadows to her left, right next to the small, elevated platform they called the stage. While everyone else mingled, drank and danced, periodically watching her sing, this guy simply watched her.

She felt his eyes on her more than anyone else in that room.

But it didn't bother her. It comforted her.

Which was kind of weird, come to think of it. His appreciative stare probably felt good because he was clearly attractive. More attractive than anyone who would ever be interested in her. Not the real—no-makeup and less sexed up—version of her anyway. It was nice to know that the deliberate seductress vibe she was putting out there was working. Perhaps it was working *too* well. She occasionally noticed seedy winks and leers from other older men in the crowd, too.

The attention, the praise, the feeling of being noticed and appreciated for the talent she finally has the opportunity to share with others was unlike anything else.

It was addictive, and she wanted more.

"Hey, that's *my* money."

"Think again, sweetheart."

Shane—the piano player—tucked the folded-up cash into his front pant pocket. The same cash he just snatched right out of Monique's hand. The money that had been paid to *her* for the performance. Of course, she intended to give him a cut. She *did* wrangle him into performing with her after all, but there was no way she was going to let him take *all* of it.

"Give the lady her money back."

A man swaggered over to them. The same guy who had been watching her from the shadows while she performed.

"What's it to you?" Shane asked with an ugly scowl that made her shudder.

"This is *my* bar mate."

"Your bar? As if some 20-year-old kid calling me 'mate' owns are bar like *this*?" Shane threw his flailing arms towards the crowded entrance of the Cyder Lounge. "Get off it! You're just a drunk. Move on and mind your own business!"

Before Monique had a moment to figure out how to snatch the cash off him, the stranger's fist thrust up and hit Shane in the chin, throwing him back. His large body landed on the concrete, unconscious beside Monique. With deliberate cool calmness, David reached down into Shane's pocket to grab the rolled-up notes and handed it to Monique.

"I believe this is *yours*. And you need a new piano player. I'll get one for you."

"Who are you exactly?"

"He's my son. David. What's going on here?" Samuel Sparks' familiar face appeared behind David.

"I hope you apologised to the lady. This is not how we conduct ourselves at this establishment. I assure you. But from what I've heard from our patrons, we need to keep you on our books. Permanently. I'd like you to come back for regular performances every Friday."

"Thank you. It would be my pleasure."

Chapter 4

David

Thnx 4 a gr8 nite. Call me x.

A message from that sexy brunette David went home with last night. Was her name Sabrina? She was nice to look at, and he got his fix, but now he was done. Too many fish in the sea to stay tied down to one girl. Contact deleted.

"Oi Dave, mate, what do you reckon we get a round of beers before we head out?"

Chris stood awkwardly beside Tony, flanked by four more familiar faces from his ever-changing entourage.

David was never alone. Chris and Tony were the constants, the core of a crew that shifted over the years. Some mates came and went, drawn in by the nightlife, the laughs, the chaos. But someone was always there to get on the piss with him, and he was grateful for it.

"Yeah bro, hold up I'll get us a round." David headed to the bar and faced Kyle's goofy face. "Six Tooheys New."

"Hey, where's *my* free drink?"

"You're working."

"How come that excuse never applies to you buddy?"

"Privilege of being a charming, top-notch bloke, mate." David scored a small chuckle from Kyle as he poured the drinks.

David involuntarily peered towards the piano and stage, eagerly waiting for Monique to perform, which should be any moment now.

"She was pretty great, huh? That Monique chick," Kyle said.

Kyle always seemed to know what David was thinking without him saying a word.

David guessed that was to be expected—they'd known each other since childhood.

Growing up together, you just understand each other.

And yet, it made David sad knowing that the friendship they once had had evaporated into thin air.

All because his so-called mate was jealous. Jealous of David's new group of friends, his legendary lifestyle, and the perks David got that Kyle couldn't access.

Of course he was jealous. Why wouldn't he be?

David almost felt sorry for him.

That's why he let Kyle live with him.

That's why he put up with the anti-social antics.

David pulled his mind back to the present, finally peeling his eyes off the stage.

"Yeah, the best," he said.

Kyle raised an eyebrow from behind the bar, halfway through pouring another schooner of Tooheys New.

"I can see where your mind's going. Leave the talent alone, would you?"

"What are you talking about?"

"You licked your lips when you said that mate. And you've been staring at the stage like she's the last woman on Earth. Don't pretend you're not imagining banging her. I get it—she's a ten. Top-tier catch. But no. Hands off."

"Why?"

"You know why."

Of course he did.

The club's reputation. His dad's reputation. And his own—already shady at best.

She was staff. Off-limits.

But somehow, that only made him want her more.

David refused to carry the drinks over to the boys. Kyle did the honours. David wasn't a server. This was *his* establishment.

Okay—technically, it was his father's. But David had been right there in the thick of it when the place transformed from a dingy dive bar into a luxurious lounge.

All that excitement, all those new opportunities and realised potential—turned to absolute shit the moment his mother left.

She walked out on both of them. For Paul.

A regular. Wealthy. One of the high-end patrons the new swanky bar was designed to attract.

And the bar transformation? It was all her idea, too. And the result? Exactly what she wanted.

Neither he nor his father had any clue that the renovation would lead to her walking out of their lives for good—leaving them broken and lost.

As he sipped his schooner at the chrome stand-up bar table, David looked around at the polished detailing: white walls with black trim, mirrored panels, hardwood floors gleaming under modern twirling teardrop chandeliers.

And there it was again—that persistent void in his gut.

Always there.

Hollowing him out behind the noise, the lights, the activity.

This place was his life.

But he feared it might be the death of him too.

Everything he saw—from the red velvet curtains he helped his mother hang to the very table where she once wiped and polished, day in, day out—made his heart ache beyond words.

So he drowned it.

He drank.

He talked shit with his mates, got them just as pissed as he was by plying them with unlimited rounds of free grog.

And he chased women. Really, really hot ones.

Probably his favourite pastime.

He couldn't deny it—he loved the chase even more than the sex.

Sure, the sex was great. But the act of chasing women other men thought were unattainable, luring them in, getting them to sleep with him—that was a euphoric elixir like no other.

Night after night, week after week, David and his boys went out on the prowl.

New prey.

Same game.

Lure in a lamb. Win the ultimate prize: her complete loss of control and restraint to him.

There was no feeling like it in the world.

Only problem was, once the prize was won and the sex was done, David had to move on.

The prey was caught.

The high achieved.

Time to hunt again.

To fill that void and avoid the pain threatening to leak out from within.

Laughter rippled around David as his mates joked and bantered, but he barely registered it. His eyes were fixed on the stage, thoughts swirling as he nursed his drink, waiting.

Then she appeared.

Monique sauntered into view—swaying hips, tousled hair catching the light just so—and his pulse kicked up a notch. He swallowed hard. She was even more of a temptress than he remembered.

And this time, the performance would be better. It had to be. That tosser of a piano player was gone, replaced by Chad—their old pianist, wrangled back in for the gig. With proper sets and songs lined up, surely Chad would do her justice.

Still, David couldn't shake the memory. She'd left the bar with that other guy. He'd hoped they'd parted ways. But maybe not. Maybe she was something more to him.

He brushed the thought aside as Monique stepped into the spotlight and began to sing.

His friends were still talking, oblivious. David threw his arms out toward them with an irritated "Shhh!" Once he had their attention, he pointed to the stage.

Monique dove deep into the lyrics of **"Too Much" by the Spice Girls**, serving up her signature blend of sass and seduction. It was like she'd cast a spell—again. The world around him faded. The noise, the crowd, the clinking glasses—all dissolved.

There was only her.

Singing to him.

She was all that mattered in this moment.

"I need her," David whispered, just loud enough for his friends to hear.

"I know you can pull some fine ladies but damn David really? She looks like she would be too hot to handle, even for you."

"Yeah plus, she's all class, mate and you are well...not."

"Shut up, Chris. What do you mean by that anyway? This is *my* bar after all."

"It's your dad's bar. Plus, you can't scrub that dive bar boy away so easily. He's still there, chugging a Tooheys New and swearing like a bogan."

David saw red at that statement, but instead of going off at him—which is what he wanted to do—he just gritted his teeth and looked away because he was right. His dad bought this place as a dingy dive bar, and he made it a real brick-and-mortar establishment for the average folk, and it thrived. But it wasn't good enough for his mum. It was her idea to transform it into what it was, and once this place that his dad loved and worked for had been turned into something he could not recognise, his mother left it all behind.

Geez, he really needed to stop thinking about that woman he once called a mother. It was nearly four years ago now, and yet somehow, she always burrowed back into his mind.

At the end of Monique's set, the guys were keen to move on to other venues for a night out, but David insisted on staying and waved them off. Hesitantly and begrudgingly, they left him behind, moping about the fact that they would not get priority entry into other clubs without him, thanks to the Cyder Lounge's excellent reputation along the strip. Too bad, so sad, they would have to deal, because tonight the only thing on his mind was Monique.

David dodged through the crowd and made his way to the side of the stage. He offered his hand like a gentleman to help her down the two steps, holding her gaze as he asked in a deliberate, seductive murmur, "May I?"

"I think I can manage to walk down two steps. But thank you for the offer."

"Okay then. Let me get you a drink. My shout."

"No, thank you. I don't drink."

David bristled at the words. He'd never heard of such a thing.

"Don't drink?"

"No. I don't."

"So, what *do* you do?"

It came out harsher than he'd intended, but it was the only question that seemed to hold the weight of all the others crowding his mind.

"How do you let loose, unwind... survive without... drinking?"

"I sing. Obviously." Her words were sharp, biting. "I don't believe drinking alcohol is a requirement for this skill set, unless you have any knowledge to the contrary?"

She looked annoyed, as if he were insinuating that she needed to be a drinker. Why couldn't she be a non-drinker? Why was that a weird thing?

Because it was weird to him. He'd only ever been surrounded by drinkers in this line of work. It was inevitable he'd become one too.

He was losing her. He'd need to turn the charm way up to get into her good books.

"Of course not. Iced water it is. I was just hoping you could stay a little while. You are drop-dead gorgeous, and your voice is something else. You deserved to be praised after that performance, and I'm more than happy to be the man to do it."

David winked. He couldn't help himself.

"Are you trying to make a pass at me? Really?"

The crinkle between her nose was damn cute, but it definitely meant she was annoyed. He was failing at this. But then she schooled her features into something resembling a pleasant, placated employee — as if remembering a role she was supposed to be playing.

"I just want to sing. Do the job your father is paying me to do and leave.

Thank you. And my audience is all the praise I'll ever need, David." David.

Not only did she know his name, but she said it. His name had never sounded so sensual, so erotic. And did her cheeks look a little more flushed than before?

Oh, she was going to be a tough nut to crack — but the cracks were there. He couldn't wait to open her up completely and get a glimpse of the woman hiding beneath.

This was shaping up to be one of his best conquests yet.

Chapter 5

Monique

"You've got the job."

Monique blinked. "What?"

"It's yours, if you want it. You know this place like the back of your hand. There's no better person."

The words landed like a slap and a hug all at once. What did that say about her? That she was the natural successor to Crazy Kathy—the woman who'd once screamed at a printer and looked like she got dressed in the dark? Probably that Monique was just as cold-faced, just as bossy, just as emotionally unavailable. The kind of woman who kept her distance from everyone in the office except Julie, who probably only tolerated her out of self-preservation. Perfect team leader material.

And wasn't that what she wanted?

Then why did it feel so... ick?

Maybe because leadership came with a wedge. Not the flimsy plastic kind she'd placed between herself and her colleagues years ago, waiting for the day she'd feel brave enough to open up. No, this was concrete. Stone. Permanent. And that day never came.

Three weeks into the new role, four weeks into her Friday night gigs at the Cyder Lounge, Monique couldn't deny it: the tail end of 1999 had catapulted her into tall poppy territory. All at once.

And now she waited for the chop. Because every poppy that grows too tall eventually gets snipped.

Her days were now a blur of quotas and call logs. She was the watcher, the enforcer. No time for slacking. Her eyes scanned the floor like Mrs Trunchbull patrolling a classroom—ready to pounce on anyone who dared step out of line. It was a strange kind of power, but it fit her better than the hamster wheel she'd been running on before. Call after call, question after question, tap after tap. Monique could already see robots doing this work one day. Hell, maybe they should.

By lunch, she escaped the office and headed up the street. She should've gone for a salad or sandwich like the other diet-obsessed women in the office, but it was Friday. The end of a long week. And she wanted a burrito. A real one. From Montezuma's—the only Mexican joint in the whole damn city.

Pant suit. Ponytail. Chunky foil-wrapped chicken burrito in hand. She rounded the corner back toward the office, waiting at the lights to cross. That's when she saw him.

David.

He wore a baggy Nike singlet and basketball shorts. His toned arms and legs were on full display, hypnotising her momentarily until she snapped back into reality. Oh no. Not like this. He couldn't see her like this.

But he wouldn't recognise her. Surely not. She looked nothing like the dolled-up version he saw on stage every Friday night. Nope. No way.

She'd cross with her head down. Fast. That should work.

The light changed. Her palms went clammy. Heart thumped. She hustled across the street, head down so far she couldn't see where she was going.

Halfway across, a hand touched her arm—gentle, but firm.

"Monique? Is that you?"

Shit. Shit. Shit.

She looked up. David's stupidly handsome face stared back at her, puzzled by her corporate disguise.

"And is that a burrito?"

"Yes," she snapped. "Now, if you'll excuse me, I'd like to get off the road. I'm not particularly keen on being hit by a car today."

How the hell did he recognise her?

She kept walking. But David didn't leave. He turned and fell into step beside her.

"What are you doing?" she asked, voice sharp.

"I'm walking with you. Where are you headed?"

"Back to my office."

"What time do you have to be back? Want to eat with me?"

He gestured toward a bench beneath a blooming jacaranda tree, nestled in a patch of greenery between the corporate towers. Suited-up city dwellers lounged there, soaking up the sun, chewing through their meagre moments of freedom.

Monique opened her mouth to tell him to take a hike—but then she saw them. Three guys and two girls from her team, heading toward the same patch of grass. They saw her. And they saw him.

They gawked.

Not at her.

At him.

And probably wondered what a guy like that was doing with a woman like her.

She had to admit—it felt good.

Why not milk it just a little?

"Okay, fine."

Over the past four weeks, Monique had slowly warmed to David's peculiar brand of charm.

After every set, he'd catch her eye—despite the chill she threw his way— and steal a few minutes to chat. He asked about her song choices, her vocal technique, and spun stories about barroom ejections and late-night escapades. Always just enough banter to stay on her radar.

It was nice, she had to admit. Having someone show genuine interest in her singing. The cold she projected didn't match the warmth she felt each time he pulled her aside. But she wouldn't let him see that. She needed the upper hand. Always.

As she performed, Monique watched how he moved through the space.

Despite the Cyder Lounge being his and his father's, David looked oddly out of place. Untethered. Almost lost. His so-called mates were clearly just hangers-on—there for the free drinks, not the friendship. Sometimes he worked the bar, sometimes the door, but mostly he floated. Free to do as he pleased. How liberating that must be.

Now here they were, seated on a bench beneath a jacaranda tree, its lavender blossoms drifting like confetti onto the cracked pavement.

"I can't believe it's you," David said. "I like corporate Monique."

"That's a lie," she scoffed.

"Not a lie at all. Now, are you going to eat that burrito or just stare at it?"

She hesitated. The thing was enormous. But now he'd called her out, she had to appear unfazed. She took a bite.

There was something about him that riled her up. She was usually cool, calm, and collected. But with David, when he baited her, she always bit.

"I can't believe you're just sitting there, watching me eat."

"I think it's my new favourite hobby."

A blush crept across her cheeks. She pivoted. "So, how old are you?"

"I turn twenty-one next month."

"Twenty-one? I'm twenty-six."

"Does our age gap bother you?"

Her cheeks flamed. She'd walked right into that one. "Why should it?"

"I don't know. You tell me."

She didn't respond. Couldn't. Instead, she focused on her burrito.

This guy—no, this *boy*—was a scrub. No doubt about it.

The chorus of **"No Scrubs" by TLC** filtered through her mind. She almost sang it to his face, just to make a point—but decided to keep her dignity intact.

David leaned back. "Now I have a question for you. That piano player who took your money—who was he to you?"

"Just some guy I slept with. No big deal."

"Wait—what?"

"I needed a piano player for my first gig at your bar. So I did what I needed to."

He stared at her. Shocked? Impressed? She couldn't tell.

"It's fine. He was pissed, but he'll get over it."

"You're not still sleeping with him, are you?"

"Of course not. I got what I needed. I'm not crazy."

"What about Chad? Our new piano player. Are you two...?"

Monique laughed. "He's already performing his role quite nicely without any extra incentive. And I have you to thank for that. So thank you."

Monique continued, flashing a grin. "Now, how about your escapades, sir? Let's delve into that dirty laundry."

"What escapades exactly?"

"I'm not blind. I see the way you flirt with the ladies. *Taken* ladies, too. Passing your number around like candy. You're sly, David. But nothing gets past me. I'm watching you."

"Yeah. And I'm watching you too—and I like what I see."

She felt the smear of sauce on her cheek as he said it. Tried to look composed. Confident.

Inside, she was anything but.

She licked it away—slow, deliberate—savouring the taste.

David rummaged through his bag and pulled out a silver digital camera, palm-sized, with a wrist strap and the word Canon gleaming across the front.

"A digital camera? How tech-savvy of you. Do you just carry that thing around?"

"Yep."

"Why? Isn't that for travel? Landmarks? Exotic locations? What in the world would be worth photographing around here?"

"Well, you. Of course. Eating a burrito. I have to show Dad. Sammy would never believe our prim and proper Monique could demolish something that size."

She'd grown fond of his father in a short time. A charmer. Like father, like son.

"Whatever. I'm owning it."

She held the burrito beside her face, deadpan, as David snapped the shot. The camera made a synthetic click. She hadn't pegged him as the photo-taking type. Turns out, he wasn't the only one surprised today.

"I didn't know you were into sports," she said, gesturing to his outfit.

"I'm a gym junkie, actually."

"Even better. Gym junkie, huh? Never heard of such a thing. What do you do at a gym, exactly? Thought that was for bodybuilders. Are you bulking up to be the next Iron Man?"

"Nah. I just run on the treadmill, pump some weights. You know. Gym stuff."

"And you do that in a room with other sweaty men? Sounds weird to me." The concept was foreign. Everyone she knew played sports or ran outside.

"How often do you go?"

"Three times a week. An hour or two each session."

"Three times a week? Where do you get the discipline? I could never."

"I need a fit bod to keep pulling beautiful ladies like you, babe. That's all the motivation I need."

Of course he winked. Of course he lifted his shirt and slapped those rock-hard abs. Such a cocky bastard.

"Don't call me babe."

"Are you sure? Your work colleagues over there seem to think the phrase fits." He threw an arm around her shoulder and waved at them.

They looked away instantly.

Turns out she wasn't the only observant one.

In that moment, Monique felt her two worlds colliding—corporate and creative—melding into one uncomfortable whole. A picture of who she was, or who she was meant to be. And she didn't like it.

She shrugged him off, glared at both David and the colleagues across the way, and stormed off.

David followed.

Once they were out of sight, he tried to speak—but Monique cut in.

"You shouldn't be here, David." Her voice was sharper than she intended. *Calm down. Stay in control. Maintain the upper hand.* She took a breath, softened. "But... thanks for keeping me company. It was... surprisingly nice. Don't expect to make a habit of it, though. This was a one-off, okay?"

"I get it. I won't pester you at your day job anymore. Goodbye, Monique.

I'll see the *real* you tonight."
     Little did he know—that wasn't the real her either.
     Not the one she truly was inside.

Chapter 6

David

"It's time to take your life more seriously."

David stared down at the enrolment forms his father had just handed him. Diploma in Hospitality Management through TAFE. The same course he'd started—and ditched—a year ago because he was above all that. Besides, he didn't need to study. He already knew how to do this shit. He lived it every day.

"I don't need a diploma to prove myself. You didn't need one either."

"Times have changed. And it's not just about a qualification. It's about building persistence and consistency. Sticking with something and seeing it through."

David's grip tightened around the papers, resisting the urge to rip them to shreds.

"Just... think about it. Okay?"

He shrugged his father off and stalked over to his loyal crew huddled around one of the tables, beers in hand.

"What was that all about?" one of them asked.

"The old man wants me to study."

"Get off it. Your dad has zero chill. Why would you want to do that? You've got it made with this setup you've got going here, mate. You don't want to lose out on all your perks."

"Bro, what I wouldn't give to trade my brickie gig for this life."

"You come and go as you want, get the ladies, and your old man gives you a consistent paycheck no matter how many hours you do—or don't—work. I wish a bit of that magic life would rub off on me."

Their reliable perspective painted a pretty great picture of his life. Why would he want to give this up? David was only twenty one. He had all the time in the world to take life seriously—and he sure as hell didn't plan on starting now.

The only person he knew who actually studied was his housemate, Kyle. Mr Law Degree. What a tosser.

David's legendary life would continue, and he had no plan to change it. But as he turned to the stage, ready to indulge in his new ritualistic obsession— watching Monique perform—he had to admit he already felt a shift within him. Just a small one, but enough to make him pause. Enough to make him wonder—briefly—if there was more to life than beers, banter, and dodging responsibility.

He'd never admit it out loud, of course. Not to his mates. Not even to himself. But something about Monique—her fire, her focus, the way she owned that stage—made his world feel a little less legendary and a little more...hollow.

He shook the thought off like wiping spilled beer off the bar—no big deal, just part of the night.

No, tonight wasn't about soul-searching. Tonight was about watching her light up the room and pretending he wasn't completely hooked.

Monique

When Monique stepped off stage, David intentionally blocked her path with a glass of chilled water in his hand, outstretched for her to take—His trademark move every week to coax her into talking to him and spending time with him. She had to give him credit—he was persistent. But it failed every time.

Until today.

Today, he bamboozled her into letting him watch her eat a burrito. Looking back on how that whole encounter unfolded, she was mortified and wanted to do everything in her power to steer clear of that man. She was dying of embarrassment knowing he even had a goofy photo of her with that damn burrito. So no, she would not be near him knowing he had seen her in her unnaturally neutral, work-safe attire.

Then, stupidly, she looked into his eyes—and that sexy-as-fuck sly smile of his.

"You must be parched. Come sit with me. Take a load off."

"Ah, umm… hmph… no. Thank you. I've got to… go."

She felt flustered. More flustered than she should appear, especially in front of him. Why did she care how he perceived her? She never cared what anyone else thought of her before. She was always able to hold that steely exterior with everyone. But around David, she could feel it wavering.

Monique brushed past him in a hurry, striding straight for the door and not looking back. She paced up the sidewalk towards the cab rank, her heels clip-clopping along. She pulled open the cab door, slid her ass into the seat and closed it.

Just as she did, the other passenger door opened.

David got in as though he'd belonged there beside her in the back of that cab. Cool, calm and casual, he even had the audacity to relax and settle in with his legs spread wide apart and his arm spread across to the centre headrest as Monique glared at him with utter astonishment.

"You are not getting in this cab with me."

"Looks like I'm already here."

"Who do you think you are? I do not need an escort…"

"I never said you needed an escort. I just want to get to know you, Monique. This seemed like the best opportunity for it."

Get to know her? Pester her, more like it.

Brazen. Bold. But damn — that level of confidence was alluring

Monique rolled her eyes.

"You right back there, darl?" The cab driver asked.

She nodded and gave him directions. He pulled away from the curb.

"Why do you want to know me?"

"Because you intrigue me."

"You're not supposed to know me. You're essentially my employer. It's a conflict of interest."

"The only conflict of interest I see is the interest you have in me."

Monique did her best to conjure up an unimpressed scowl to hide the blush blooming in her cheeks.

"Come on now, don't give me that look. I know you want to know more about me too. You're just trying to hide it. And failing at it too, I might add."

"I already know who you are. I see how you mingle with the crowd while you pretend to work and flirt with the girls."

"So you watch me, huh? Glad to know the whole watching thing isn't one-sided. You obviously notice then how much I watch you too. While you perform. You are so distracting, Monique. You are the one keeping me away from... my essential tasks."

David ran his thumb across his lower lip, his stare burrowing right through her.

"Your tasks don't seem that essential," Monique scoffed.

"You're right. You're the only essential thing in that room."

Somehow, his face sat a mere breath away from hers. Had he moved closer—or had she? Each word shared between them felt like a magnet, drawing them together. Involuntary. Unnoticed. Yet unavoidable.

"I need you, Monique."

His thumb traced the curve of her jaw, the slight touch sending shivers across her skin.

"Don't..." The word caught in her throat, her mind and heart warring over what to say next.

David stilled, his slow caress halting.

"Don't... stop."

"Beautiful Stranger" by Madonna played on the radio, scorching the electric desire radiating between them, pushing her need for him beyond breaking point. And she couldn't deny the need reflected in his steely gaze either.

In that moment, her open mouth fell into his, and like a taut tether snapping, they were on each other like two dogs on heat. Arms, lips, mouths. The way she absolutely consumed this man in the back seat of that cab—and the way he devoured her—Monique felt like a giddy teenager, discovering the thrill of kissing for the first time.

But oh lord, he said he needed her. And right now, in this moment, she felt it. Every inch of that need. She had completely thrown her hat in on holding back the desire she'd tried to bury ever since she laid eyes on him.

The cab stopped at her house.

It wasn't until that moment that she realised the show they had probably put on for the cab driver.

As Monique stepped out of the car, David did too.

"You are not coming into my house, David. I will not be another notch in your belt. I'm too good to be a one-night stand."

"I don't deny that. I'm just walking you to your door. Like the gentleman that I am."

"Oi! What do you think you're doing here?"

As they walked side by side up her driveway, Monique looked up to see Shane sitting on the bottom step of her front door.

"I could ask you the same question." Shane stood up and started walking towards them.

"Oh don't tell me you're sleeping with this guy now? What a fucking laugh!"

Before David had a chance to respond, Monique cut in.

"Shane, I told you not to come back here. You got your money, and I told you—we're done."

"We're done when I say we're done. You don't get to drop me like I'm nothing."

"But you are nothing, Shane. Geez! What did you think we were exactly, huh? A couple? Ha! I slept with you twice, Shane, and the sex wasn't even good."

"You fucking bitch."

Shane rushed at Monique, but she stood her ground just as David stepped between them.

"Back off and fuck off, would you, or I'm gonna have to knock you out again. We both know what an embarrassing scene that was last time."

Shane threw his hands up in the air with a defensive stance.

"Okay. Fine. I'll go."

As Shane started to walk past them, as if to leave, he threw a heavy right hook directly into David's cheek, sending him stumbling back into Monique's arms.

"Now we're even."

Chapter 7

David

He should have seen that punch coming from a mile away, but when he fell back and landed in Monique's soft arms, smelling of roses, he figured that surge of pain was worth it. Her arms stayed around him, soothing and comforting him as she led him into her townhouse to get a cold pack. If a punch in the face was all it took for Monique to soften around him, he might consider seeking out a reason to be assaulted more often.

"You need to lie down."

She turned on her radio, pulled an ice pack from the fridge, wrapped it in a tea towel, and gave it to David. He pressed it to his cheek, the coolness quickly soothing the sharp sting. He followed her past the lounge room and past the fake leather-studded couch sitting in the centre—clearly purchased for aesthetics rather than comfort—before she shuffled him towards her... bedroom?

The space was so small, this appeared to be the only bedroom. She must live alone.

Once he walked through the tinkling gold bead curtains hanging from the top of the doorway, the room struck him as being very Monique. This wasn't a bedroom. It was a boudoir. Black walls. Dim mood lighting from the bedside lamps, Monique turned on by simply touching the base of them with her finger. In the centre sat a plush queen bed covered in animal print designs, backed by a textured dark maroon feature wall and a gold smiling sun sculpture hanging in the centre.

To the left sat her wardrobe, with what looked to be a framed collage of some sort hanging on the wall next to it, covered in cutouts of singers and travel destinations.

"You like to travel, huh?" David asked.

"Haven't done any yet. But I'd like to. One day."

On the right side of the room sat an ornate vanity table, spray-painted in gold and covered with perfumes, makeup, candles and... troll dolls?

He walked over to a framed photo sitting on her dresser and held it up for a closer look.

"Is that your mum?" David asked.

"Yeah."

"She looks a lot like you."

"I guess so... She's dead, by the way."

"Oh shit, sorry."

"It's been over a year now and I still miss her. How about your mum? How come I never see her at the club?"

"I don't want to talk about it," David bit out, as if it were the only way his mouth could consider spitting out a response to that question. He flinched, regretting his tone, especially after seeing a look of shock and pity cross Monique's face. This was not the vibe he wanted to sit in right now. He had to push that topic off a steep cliff and lighten the mood.

"Now I do want to talk about this ugly-looking thing." David picked up a troll doll by the pointed tip of its hot pink hair and raised an inquisitive brow. "A Troll Doll? Really?"

"How dare you," Monique said with mock offence, snatching it out of his hand and placing it back on the vanity. "They are adorable, and I won't hear a bad word said about them. Now lie down, will you?"

He would not let her get away with that one. He needed to reel her in and keep her there.

"Is that a request or a command?"

He didn't wait for her response. He kicked off his shoes, lifted the bed covers, and slid into the warm, tightly tucked bed sheets, making himself comfortable and placing the cold pack down on the bedside table. He knew the game he was playing. It was a dangerous one with risks, but the lure of her—after getting a taste of her—was too much to resist.

Monique

"Don't go turning this into something it's not."

What a cocky fuck. She needed to shut this down now, all while subsequently hating herself for requesting him to lie in her bed. What was she thinking?

David's arrogantly handsome grin widened into a beaming smile as he tucked both hands behind his head.

"So, you're telling me this is not how you seduced guys like Shane into bed with you? Bringing me into your bedroom was your idea. Remember?"

"Shane was a... mistake. And I'm getting the feeling this was a mistake too."

"It certainly didn't feel like a mistake in the back of that taxi."

Was it getting hot in here? Her cheeks burned, because what they did in that taxi was spontaneous, unexpected, and downright delicious—but there was no way she wanted him to know that.

"Whatever is going on here can't happen. I will not become a random woman that falls into bed with you. I know your reputation."

David's eyes darkened. "I'm not going to deny it. What can I say? I love women. Is that so bad?"

"You don't love women. You use them."

"And you don't do the same to men?"

"Touche."

David flexed, the muscles in his arms taut as he propped himself up on his elbows. A slow grin spread across his face.

"Seems to me like we're a perfect match."

"Match from hell."

"A match is still a match."

Monique tipped her head down closer to his.

"I don't match. With anyone. And neither do you, it seems. A match is... messy."

"Then use me," he said, voice low and steady. "I can take it. And I intend to use up every inch of you too."

David raked his gaze over her body, slow and deliberate, his teeth pressing into his lower lip.

"I hate your fucked-up logic."

"No you don't."

David tapped the mattress beside him—still deliciously handsome despite the shiner on his cheek—and whispered, "Come over here."

Monique realised David was mimicking the sensual words in the song playing on the radio out in the living room—**"Need You Tonight" by INXS.**

"What makes you think you're calling the shots here in my house?"

Monique stood next to the bed, her arms crossed over her chest as she looked down at David. He was lying in her bed, looking up at her with a cocky grin. He was trying to seduce her, but she was determined to resist.

"Come on, Monique," he said, his voice low and husky. "You know you want to."

Monique shook her head, silently willing her logical brain to overcome her treacherous heart, but the sight of him lying in her bed and wanting her so badly raised serious doubts about her brain's ability to win this one.

David pulled his black T-shirt up and over his head, revealing tanned abs and perfectly sculpted biceps.

"Are you afraid of what I might do to you?"

Monique hesitated for a moment before finally admitting, "I'm afraid that you severely overestimate yourself."

"Then let me prove you wrong."

Monique should know better than to trust a man like David. He was a player, and she would just be another conquest to him. But the thought of having a piece of him sent a thrill through her that she could not hide. Yes, she knew his reputation, but perhaps he was right. Maybe a one-off fling with no strings attached was exactly what she needed. Emotionally distant and one hundred percent physical. That was something she could rationalise.

As for her singing career, as long as this stayed between them and was only a one-time thing, she could pull down her barriers. But she had to gain the upper hand. She wouldn't allow herself to be completely defenceless against his charms, so she wrapped her hand around his neck, pulled his head up to hers, and kissed him passionately.

She reached into the drawer beside the bed and pulled out a condom, holding it up between them like a contract. "This stays between us, got it? Don't make me regret this."

David gently wrapped his hand around her waist and pulled her down onto the bed, his expression hungry and wanting.

David's lips found hers again, and Monique was lost in the moment, sinking deeper into the intoxication of him. He was a good kisser. Really good. She knew she was playing with fire, but she didn't care. All that mattered was the feel of David's body against hers and the way he made her feel alive.

Monique let herself sink into the kiss, her fingers threading through his hair as if holding on for dear life or she'd drown in him. His hand slid along her waist—not possessive, but reverent—like he was memorising the shape of her.

She felt the heat between them rise, but it wasn't just lust—it was the ache of wanting someone who might never be safe to want.

They moved together with a kind of urgency that wasn't rushed, just inevitable. Every touch was a question, every sigh an answer. Monique let herself be undone—not by his reputation or the thrill of rebellion—but by the way he felt inside her, on her, and the way he looked at her like she was the only truth he'd ever known.

She didn't need promises. Just this moment. Just this night.

And when it was over—when their bodies stilled and the silence wrapped around them like a secret—Monique lay there, her cheek against his chest, listening to the steady rhythm of a man who had somehow made her forget the rules she'd written for herself.

She didn't know what tomorrow would bring. But for now, she let herself believe that maybe, just maybe, she hadn't made a mistake.

David

David grasped the door handle, his head resting against the wood. It was 6 a.m., and he was not ready to come home to the inevitable slagging from Kyle. The front door creaked as he opened it and stepped inside.

"You dirty dog."

"What?" David hung his head low, avoiding eye contact.

"You know what. You slept with Monique, and you stayed the night. Since when do you stay the night?"

He couldn't deny it. The sex he'd had with Monique last night was, in fact, as good as the chase—if not better. But Kyle would never know that, so instead he said, "I uh, fell asleep. No big deal."

"This is a big deal, bro. What did I say? Hands off the employee!"

"What makes you think you can tell me what I can and can't do? Just because you're getting some damn degree, it doesn't make you better than me."

"What's that got to do with anything? I'm just trying to protect your dad's business. Something you should probably be doing, bud."

Kyle was there for all of it—the lows, the highs, and everything that came with the transformation of The Cyder Lounge and their lives. But he was on the outside looking in. He wasn't in the middle of the family dramas, so he could never really understand.

"Don't you dare assume I don't give a shit about my dad."

David held back from including The Cyder Lounge in that statement, because he hadn't entirely decided if he was as protective of that place. His feelings for it were complicated, to say the least.

David continued, "And Monique and I? It was just sex. No strings attached. It won't change a thing."

Kyle took a long sip of his coffee, as if the caffeine hit might help him digest David's words.

"And what about your diploma? Your dad told me he wants you to finish it. So, are you gonna do it?"

"I don't need to do shit," David bit back.

He had just six months left to finish it when he abandoned it a year ago and quit his studies for good.

"And there lies the problem."

There was that disappointed look again. The same one he'd been seeing from those he cared about too often lately. David swallowed hard. He should have felt angry, but he was hurt—and even a bit ashamed.

Before he had a chance to respond, Kyle picked up his cap and sunnies before heading to the front door David had just walked through. Typical Kyle, heading out for his early morning run looking fresh as a daisy, while David probably looked like he'd taken a literal roll in a bale of hay.

Kyle approached him, standing toe to toe, his face so close David could see the tenseness in his jaw and the deep-set crinkle in his brow.

"You can't live this way forever. Getting around carefree and fucking shit up along the way. One day, something is gonna give—and you'll regret that you weren't man enough to step up to the plate."

Chapter 8

David

"You never called me back."

David thought he'd recognised her. Had he slept with her? Yes. He had. That sex was mediocre at best. What was her name again?

"Well?"

Oh right, she actually wanted a response. Did her name start with an S?

"Sabrina. Honey. There you are!"

An ugly, balding bloke called out from behind her, drawing her attention away from the bar. Yep, that's it. Sabrina. Her knight in balding glory could not have come a moment too soon, thankfully allowing him to avoid a very awkward conversation.

This was definitely the downside to his fetish for one-night stands. There would always be someone looking for more than he was willing to give.

That fact would never change, and Monique was no exception. He had seen many former conquests sweep into his bar and barely gave them a second glance, so he knew he could keep things at a distance with Monique now. He'd done it so many times before.

As David fell into the usual routine of serving drinks, from the corner of his eye he noticed Maggie—a short, blonde, middle-aged lady with a bob cut and glasses, her small frame hefting a heavy box as big as her torso. She barely made her way through the door before his father whisked over from

God knows where and swooped the box out of her arms.

Another wrong delivery, it seemed.

Maggie owned a quaint bar called *Sips and Stories*, where people drank grog while reading books or listening to authors—or avid readers—read stories out loud. Sounded like a snore to him. Not David's scene at all.

Her address was 7 Banks Street, while The Cyder Lounge was 17 Banks Street. Because posties obviously can't read, turns out some of their deliveries ended up at her establishment, and she was always kind enough to deliver them here in person. In fact, it had happened so often recently, David almost considered her a regular.

"Howz business, Maggie?" he heard his father say as they both approached the bar where David stood.

"Oh, you know, I'm getting by. Could be better. Could be worse."

"I see, I see. Well, I commend you for doing something unique. Gotta take risks in this business to stand out, and that takes guts. If you need help, I'm happy to share drink vouchers from your joint at my establishment. You know—to spread the word. Get more patrons through your doors."

"Oh really? Thank you, Sammy. You're too kind."

Sammy? David could have sworn he saw a blush creep up his father's face.

As Maggie waved goodbye and headed out the door, David followed his dad into the back room to store the box of whiskey glasses.

"Dad, you know our patrons aren't the right fit for her joint."

"You never know, son. There could be a few bookworms amongst this lot. Plus, I'm just trying to help the nice lady out."

"What happened to not mixing business with pleasure?"

"I do not know what you are talking about. Our relationship is purely professional. Now you, on the other hand—I've seen you making eyes at our new performer, Monique. We've been pulling more numbers on Friday nights since she started performing, and I don't want you ruining that for us. Got it?"

All David could do was give his dad a curt nod. He refused to say a word, because whatever he said would be a lie. He'd already crossed that line, and despite the risk, he didn't regret it—and he was determined to make sure his father would never find out about it either.

Monique

The nerves wrestling in Monique's gut tonight had nothing to do with her upcoming performance—and everything to do with David. That beautiful scoundrel who seduced her into sleeping with him. After that wild night, they both agreed it would be nothing more. One and done. From here on in, they would purely be work acquaintances.

So why wouldn't her nerves settle?

"Hey, after our set, wanna grab a bite to eat?"

Chad, the new piano player David found for her, was a young, sweet man who was an absolute delight to perform with. No trouble at all, and excellent at following her lead. They hadn't really socialised outside of the live performances, and she had nothing better to do after the gig, so she said, "Sure."

When she stepped onto the stage, Monique inadvertently made eye contact with David behind the bar right away—then looked away, forcing herself not to glance in his direction again for her entire performance. If she ever felt the urge to look at him again, she made herself look over at Chad instead.

As always, the applause, wolf whistles, and cheers made her face beam and her heart swell. She was encouraged to see more and more patrons each time she came to perform. Then, as she looked across to the back of the bar, she noticed two young, skinny things in figure-hugging dresses feeling up David's flexed bicep as if he were putting on a one-man show just for them while he served their drinks.

Disgusting. Seeing those girls fawn over that schmuck made her want to vomit in her mouth.

"Are we good to go? I've got a great place in mind."

"I've just got to go freshen up first. I'll be out in a sec.

David

"Show us your muscles and I'll give you a nice tip!"

How could he refuse? He never turned down an offer to get the guns out—especially for admirers so fine. But as the song ended and he looked up to see Monique shooting daggers at him with her eyes, his first instinct was to recoil, like he'd done something wrong.

But he hadn't done anything wrong. This was who he was. Monique knew that, and he'd given her fair warning. Didn't stop him from wanting to talk to her after her set, though. To make sure everything was still cool between them, of course. Nothing more.

But instead of finding Monique, he was faced with Chad.

"Guess who I'm going on a date with tonight?"

That cocky grin didn't really fit this scrawny, unassuming bloke who was about as bland as a brick wall. David let out a huff, not hiding the fact he was uninterested in hearing the answer. He barely talked to the guy, so God knows why he wanted to tell him.

"I don't know, maestro. You tell me."

"Monique."

If David hadn't swallowed the swig of beer he'd gulped down earlier, he would have spat it out all over Chad.

He had the biggest shit-eating grin on his face too, the kind that made David's blood boil.

"Is that so?" David managed to spit out between gritted teeth. "And why are you telling me this?"

"You're not the only one who can get the girls around here."

"How do you know I haven't already had a slice of that pie?"

David winked with an even bigger shit-eating grin and walked away before he got a response.

Shit. Why did he do that? He wasn't supposed to let whatever happened between them slip, but as usual, his pride and ego had to get the better of him.

"Telling Everybody" by Human Nature began playing over the bar's speakers. Of course it did.

He didn't want to hang around to get any more gory details about whatever those two were about to get up to, because he could already feel his blood boiling. He shouldn't be this angry.

He grabbed another beer and busied himself wiping down the bench—anything to cool the flames of jealousy flaring in his gut as Chad and Monique strolled past towards the door. His leg muscle twitched like it had a mind of its own, plotting Chad's downfall—literally—but he settled for scrubbing imaginary spots with newfound intensity instead.

Chapter 9

Monique

Monique bit down into the deliciously flaky, rich, gravy-filled meat pie, with a squirt of tomato sauce added to each bite. Not exactly the kind of dinner she expected, but Chad did say "a bite to eat," and pies fit that description perfectly.

This was nice. Eating out with someone with no other intentions or ulterior motives tied to it. It was almost like having a friend.

Was Chad her friend now?

"So, uh... wanna head to my place after this?" Chad said suggestively, with an awkward wink that looked like a poor copy of one out of David's playbook.

Welp. Guess she was wrong about that. Dead wrong. How did they go from talking about their music tastes and the potential longevity of a weird online store selling books called *Amazon* to "hey, wanna root?"

"No, Chad. I'm not that kind of girl."

"David told me that you are that kind of girl—and he already had his shot with you."

He wouldn't. He didn't.

Monique's skin flamed so hot, if she spat in Chad's face, she wouldn't be surprised if her seething saliva burned his skin.

"Did he now?"

"How come he gets to shoot his shot with you and not me?"

"What makes you think I would let that man—or any other man, for that fact—get within breathing room of me?"

It was a big, fat lie, but one she threw herself into with full sincerity.

"I am not some piece of meat to be passed around."

Monique practically spat the words out as she stood up and grasped her clutch, ready to bolt.

"Okay, okay. Cool it, would ya? Let's just pretend this never happened, yeah? I must've misread the signals, that's all."

It was always her fault. Never theirs. She was the one putting out the "have sex with me" vibes—through her clothes, the way she talked, moved, and existed. They were never in the wrong for assuming they could take what they wanted. Ever.

She should have never let David take what he wanted from her. This is how she got hurt.

Her mother was right.

Her mother, Catherine Chambers, was a strong, hard-working single mother who never let a man take advantage of her and provided for them both on her own. Monique wanted to be just like her. At times while performing, she even imagined seeing her in the crowd, proud mama bear cheering her on.

She was the only one who pushed her to chase her dreams, well before she even had the confidence to do it herself. And she hated that it took her mother's sudden death to finally go after what she wanted—and deserved—in life.

Her dream to travel was all thanks to her too. Ever since she was a child, her mother told tall tales of all the adventures they'd go on in foreign lands together, once they had enough money to do it. But that day never came. And Monique was determined to live out that dream for the both of them.

But here, in this moment—with another man treating her as less than human, all because David had the audacity to gloat about her being just another conquest—she could feel her mother's judgment and shame.

This was not the strong, independent woman she raised. The kind of woman that gets taken advantage of by a man. She was taught to be the one taking advantage of them. It was the only way a woman could survive and thrive in this world.

Tears fell out of nowhere, and Monique could not hold back the waterworks. She had to turn and leave before Chad noticed the weakness her eyes were betraying.

She would not let a man be the cause of eroding her self-esteem.

Especially not David.

David

"I'm gonna fuck you so hard you won't remember your name," David whispered into miss blondie's ear in the back of the cab—just as **"Say My Name" by Destiny's Child** pulsed through the speakers. Ironic timing. Considering he'd already forgotten hers, it would be a blessing if she forgot his too—just in case he let the wrong name slip.

When they arrived at his place, David practically tumbled out of the car, his head spinning and legs tripping over themselves. But somehow, he still managed enough quality one-liners and charisma to convince this sweet blonde thing to come home with him. He needed this—to clear his head and forget himself. Maybe if the pleasure was intense enough, he'd forget his own name, too.

He barely made it two steps up the driveway before he saw a familiar silhouette leaning against the brick wall of his house beneath a dimly lit porch light.

"Get back in the cab."

"Who is she?" Miss blondie said from behind him.

"Go home or... go find someone else to fuck. I don't care."

She was confused, clearly, so David turned around and gently persuaded her back into the cab, shut the door, and handed the driver a fifty to take her wherever she wanted to go. Whatever he had planned for that night died in its tracks at the sight of Monique on his doorstep.

Before David got a chance to say anything, something hard hit his chest and fell to the floor. A leopard print clutch?

By the time he looked up, Monique was in his face, her expression filled with fury.

"You told him. How dare you!"

She was in his face now, full of rage.

"Who else did you tell?"

"No one," David said, somewhat sheepishly.

"I don't believe you."

"I didn't want to tell anyone. I still don't. But Chad... fuck. I didn't mean to. I couldn't help it."

"You needed someone to gloat to about your conquest. Is that it? Like I'm some kind of prize to be won?"

He didn't want to admit this to her—let alone to himself. But it was the truth, and the truth seemed to be the only clear path out of this mess.

"It wasn't supposed to be like this, damnit. I didn't want to fucking care..."

"Care about what?"

You. That was the first word that flashed in his mind, but he refused to say it out loud. He couldn't admit that to her—let alone himself.

"Chad told me he was taking you on a date. I didn't like that, so I said what I said. I regret it, but I can't take it back. All I can do is apologise. Let me make it up to you."

"That's a bit rich coming from a man who brought another pretty little thing home to bang right in front of me."

"You were not supposed to be here, and you already know that this is what I do. I didn't think you cared about who I slept with."

Monique stood silently, appearing to contemplate his words, the fire cooling in her eyes.

"Plus, I made her leave because I wanted you to stay."

David couldn't deny that the feeling he was trying to suppress with another one-night stand evaporated the moment he laid eyes on Monique—as if she alone were his ultimate cure. That realisation was equal parts astounding and terrifying. Tingles rippled through his body as he drank in her beauty, her sincerity, and the raw emotion levelled squarely at him.

"Now I could be wrong, but maybe I'm not the only one who cares here. I saw the way you looked at those girls at the bar who wanted to cop a feel."

"Oh, please. If anything, I felt sorry for them—for having to put up with your pompous antics."

"And why did you come to my house to tell me off in person? How did you even find out where I lived?"

"Kyle was very forthcoming. And I... needed you to know that you cannot talk about me in that way, or I'll never step foot into The Cyder Lounge again. For business or pleasure. Do you understand?"

He knew that performing on stage meant a lot to Monique, so knowing she would walk away from it because of him and the things he said made him feel like shit.

"I understand, and I'm sorry. I didn't mean to hurt you."

"How can I make it up to you? I'll get down on my knees if I have to."

David literally got to his knees and lay his head at her feet like some kind of dog. He had never stooped that low for anyone—but for Monique, it felt like the appropriate amount of grovelling to get back into her good graces.

As he looked up at her, he was delighted to see her biting her lower lip, which gave him more than enough permission to run his hands up her silky smooth thighs.

As David's hands trailed higher, he asked, "Do you want me to stop?"

"No," she whispered. "I think you know what to do. You can consider this your apology."

She peered down at him with a wicked smile that would have made a younger, more inexperienced version of himself come in his pants.

"My pleasure."

He licked and teased her clit like it were a lemon merengue, soft, delicate and delicious. Monique didn't hold back—her moans were long, decadent, and irresistible. Just as David pulled her panties aside and slipped two fingers inside her wet opening, the heavens opened up. It began to pour—hard, loud, fast, and very, very wet. Just like her.

Rather than sending them fleeing for cover, the downpour only seemed to fuel her path toward ecstasy, adding a whole other sensual layer to this erotic experience in the place he least expected it—on the front driveway of his house.

When Monique climaxed, her legs quivering and clenching around his face and fingers, he pulled away—pleased for her, while also harnessing a throbbing erection of his own.

"What does a girl have to do to get an umbrella around here?" Monique said with an elaborate sigh.

"Thank you for the apology. I think that would suffice. Pffew, well I'm beat. I'd better call a cab and head home to bed."

Looking into David's eyes, then down at his bulging erection threatening to burst out, and back up at his face with a smirk, she added, "You don't mind, do you?"

"Not at all."

Fair play, Monique. Fair play.

Of course he wanted to be buried deep inside her in that moment, but he'd be wrong to expect it after how his words had hurt her. In fact, he was still in shock that he'd ended up in this kind of situation with her again—and he was more than happy to do all that he needed to do to get back to where he wanted to be with her.

Especially if it involved extracurricular activities like this.

In fact, this chase—with her and only her—to get back into her good books could be enough to satisfy his cravings for a while. And perhaps, if they were to keep it between themselves for real this time, maybe it wasn't such a bad thing to keep this good thing they had going... for a little while longer.

Chapter 10

Monique

"Hey Monique, wanna grab a bite to eat?"

Her only office friend, Julie, had been warming up to her again recently after the ice-cold shoulder she'd given her following Monique's promotion. For the past few weeks, she'd only shared formal, work-only conversations with her—as if being her inferior made it too awkward for Julie to have a real conversation anymore. Monique found it strange, but she'd accepted it as a consequence of her new role and moved on with her life.

That was until Julie came into the office with a cupcake to share last week and, out of nowhere, started dishing out office gossip again. It was like she'd been let back into that coveted workplace social circle she thought she'd been barred from since becoming a manager. Despite the occasional friendly banter in the office, this was the first time Julie had asked her to lunch. And as nonchalantly as she could muster—despite the giddy joy bubbling inside her—Monique answered, "Sure."

Monique sat, staring at the pitiful garden salad she'd purchased from the sandwich and salad bar. Julie was still waiting in line. She would have preferred hot chips smothered in gravy, but she wouldn't dare while in Julie's company. She could feel Julie's silent judgment whenever she ate anything remotely unhealthy. She felt the same judgment from a large portion of the women in the office, actually—as if they were all in some kind of silent contest to devour the blandest, greenest item on any menu.

She didn't usually partake in the depressing contest. She told herself she didn't care about their judgment—but she obviously did, because here she was, forcing down a forkful of wilted leaves that did nothing to satisfy her ravenous hunger. Simply because Julie was sitting with her today.

While she waited, sipping her water, she peered at the others sitting around the park eating. Some were chatting, two blokes were reading the newspaper, one woman had her head tucked into a novel—but she also noticed a strange new trend during break time that had become more common lately: people with their faces glued to their phones.

She noticed one man completely zoned out of the conversation around him, staring at his Nokia. Probably playing Snake or sending a text message. It was only back in his pocket for a few moments before it pinged, and he pulled it out again, tapping away at the numbers with his thumbs. Yep—definitely a text message. Once that thing was in his palm, he had no care in the world for the real people sitting beside him.

The fast rise of mobile phones and their infiltration into society both excited and unsettled her. Monique had her own mobile phone—she'd bought it a year ago from a Telstra shop—and she already couldn't imagine living without it. Still, she felt an ominous sense of foreboding. Now that this technology was in the world, there was no going back. Somehow, she knew that she—and everyone else—would be spending more time staring at those little screens, distracted from the real world around them, for far longer than anyone could anticipate.

"You're not really eating that, are you?"

Monique damn near jumped out of her skin to find David sitting down next to her.

"Uh, yes, I am. What are you doing here?"

"Just finished up at the gym, noticed you sitting here and decided to join. Here, you can have this."

He tossed a Snickers bar into her lap as he began to unwrap one of his own.

"You're not eating that for lunch, are you?"

"No…" he drawled, flashing a guilty look before taking a big bite. Such a juvenile.

"Well, hello there."

Monique looked up to see Julie flashing a tight smile at them both, purse and salad wrap in hand.

"May I take a seat? My name is Julie," she said to David, barely acknowledging Monique at all.

"Oh hey, I'm David. Sorry—I didn't know you had a friend with you today."

Rather than sitting next to Monique, Julie slid comfortably into the seat beside David.

"And Monique didn't tell me she had a boyfriend."

"He's not my boyfriend," Monique blurted so fast she nearly choked on some spinach in the process.

"No, I'm a... friend. I better go. I'll see you tonight," David said as he stood, pointing to Monique with a sly grin before turning to Julie. "Now why haven't I seen you at The Cyder Lounge?"

Before Monique had a chance to interject with something like, *Oh, she wouldn't be interested,* or *That place is littered with asbestos,* anything to deter her from The Cyder Lounge—Julie responded:

"Well, I've never been invited."

"Well, consider yourself invited. It's going to be a great show."

"Great, count me in!" Julie replied in a sing-song tone Monique had never heard from her before.

"See you both tonight."

David flashed his signature wink, smile, and twinkle in his eye before walking away.

Monique could have died on the spot.

Julie didn't know Monique performed there—and she didn't want her to know either. David had just inadvertently exposed her best-kept secret, the one that kept her two worlds from colliding.

As David walked away, Julie proceeded to grill her about him and what they were doing at The Cyder Lounge that night. But Monique stayed tight-lipped, offering short, clipped answers that gave nothing away. She needed time to figure a way out of this. She had to. If her work colleagues saw her as some slutty stage performer in a nightclub, how would any of them take her seriously? She was their manager, for Christ's sake. Exposing this side of herself felt like exposing her biggest vulnerability—opening herself up to endless ridicule and failure.

She needed to find a way out of this. And fast.

But this situation wasn't the only one she needed to handle.

She had to do something about David.

She looked down at the Snickers bar he'd given her before tucking it into her black leather handbag.

He kept doing things like this. Things that made her feel like he cared.

But he didn't care for her. Not really.

The only person who ever truly cared for her was her mother—and that role was reserved solely for her. No one else deserved the title of being someone who cared for her. And her heart sank, knowing her mother was dead and that she'd never be cared for like that again.

He even said that he cared. Like it was no big deal. A fact as benign as the price of bread.

But it meant nothing. Not to a roguish boy like him, set in his ways—the local fuckboy for the girlfriends and wives of the elite who frequented his father's establishment. No, he didn't care. The only person he really cared about was himself.

And that's why she had to end it. Somehow.

But she had to do it in a way that let her keep her job at The Cyder Lounge without making things awkward between them in the future. She convinced herself this was what they both wanted. Someone needed to be the catalyst for a clean break, and it may as well be her. She'd orchestrated so many others in the past and come out the other end relatively unscathed.

And she'd do it again.

Chapter 11

Monique

Monique's hands shook more than they ever had in her whole life—knowing who she was likely to find in that bar tonight, and knowing what that would lead to. It didn't help that things had ended on a sour note with Chad the week prior. They hadn't spoken since she refused his inappropriate proposition.

But as she walked through the glass doors of The Cyder Lounge and made her way past the crowd toward the stage, the situation was even worse than she'd imagined.

Way worse.

Not only did she find Julie sitting at one of the tables near the front of the stage, but nearly half the bloody office was crowded around the table with her. They were all laughing and shouting, clearly half-sloshed and not remotely aware of who they were about to see on stage. Not at all. They probably expected Monique to be there at the table with them.

But how did they all end up here?

Julie had jumped at the chance to go to the exclusive Cyder Lounge, as Monique expected she would—despite her failed attempts to dull Julie's starry-eyed enthusiasm about the joint. Being the gossip hound she was, Julie had probably bragged to everyone about it and invited them along for a night out. It made sense. They often went out on the town together on Friday nights.

Monique should have considered herself lucky they hadn't wandered into this bar already, but she knew the pricey entry fee and liquor probably kept them away.

Until now.

She could see the black VIP drink vouchers on the table—David must have given them out. He probably thought he was being nice. Probably thought he'd earn brownie points for inviting them in and seating her "friends" right in front of the stage for front-row seats to her show.

Oh, how wrong he was.

She should have told him. Should have made him revoke the invite. But she couldn't bring herself to do it.

But they were here now. And so was she.

As much as she wanted to walk away, she also didn't want to let David and Samuel down. She prided herself on being reliable, and she would face one of her biggest fears to ensure that stayed intact.

Monique sucked in a deep breath, shook out her nerves, and turned the performer in her on.

When she was being someone else up there on stage, they couldn't hurt her. Because it wasn't really her up there. It was a character. A role she was playing.

And she played it damn well.

But knowing that didn't stop her from noticing the shock written across the faces of her colleagues. Julie's mouth gaped so wide she could have swallowed her wine glass. Derrick, Carl, and Lucy all wore similar expressions.

David happened to walk over to their table to clear away glasses—probably to get a closer look at how Monique would react to them being there. Her nervous expression was probably not what he expected.

Then Julie started laughing. Full-on belly laughing. Like this was all some big joke.

David looked down at her in pure disgust just as Derrick let out a long wolf whistle and yelled:

"Let's go, Money Mon! Show us what you've got, baby!"

She had a nickname? Just like Crazy Kathy did?

She'd never heard it before, but the name made sense—since she always toed the company line, valuing more money coming in over pretty much everything else. That's what she was paid to do, after all.

Everything in her body told her to back down. Walk away. Never step foot on that stage again.

But she was not weak.

Her mother taught her better.

She tried her best to picture her mother—standing in the back, smiling and cheering her on. She used her as motivation to push forward and sing **"Breathe" by Kylie Minogue**.

And she kept singing.

Until the crowd around her faded away, and everything she let out of her mouth and her heart was to be solely shared between her and her mother.

Everyone else were mere inconsequential spectators.

David

Once Monique started singing, the whole place went silent, like it usually did when she launched into a beautiful ballad like this one, and thankfully the laughter and whispered judgements from Monique's so-called friends subsided. If they hadn't, he was that close to kicking them out of his bar.

Perhaps there was a reason Monique never invited them here.

She had never told them about this.

Who she was in this place.

An ominous dread filled his gut at the realisation. Had he just set her up for ridicule and embarrassment at her work? That was not his intention. Surely, she'd understand that. But he knew this was another strike against him, and he'd already had one too many.

As Monique continued into her second song, he noticed the expressions on their faces transform from mockery into wonder and awe. And so they should. She deserved nothing less.

Monique

"I'm sorry, I didn't know," David managed to whisper into Monique's ear as she stepped off stage—just before she was surrounded by her colleagues.

"Wow, Monique. Look at you! You look like a completely different person. And you can sing? Since when could you sing like that? You've been holding out on us!" said Carl.

"Just wait until Janice finds out about this," Derrick added.

Janice. The office manager. Oh no. She couldn't know. This was bad enough, but her boss finding out was a whole other level Monique didn't want to deal with.

Julie must have seen the colour drain from her face, because she said, "Janice doesn't need to know. I think we keep this between us."

After the show, Monique sat and actually enjoyed the company of her colleagues for the first time. She felt a warmth and genuine friendliness from them she'd never experienced before—even from Julie—as they laughed and shared little pieces of themselves and their lives outside of work with her.

And it was really, really nice.

Perhaps David actually had done her a solid here, in a roundabout way.

But once their group decided to move on to the Embassy Nightclub to hit the dancefloor, Monique wished them a wonderful night and planned to stay behind. She needed to talk to David.

But when she noticed a very sober-looking David chatting with Kyle at the bar while cleaning glasses, she chickened out.

What could have been a god-awful night had turned out to be a good one, and she didn't want to ruin it now. So she walked out of the bar with every intention of heading home.

But her mind kept pulling her back to David.

David

David glanced at the clock. It was 1 a.m. already? He'd been so busy pouring drinks and serving patrons that the night had gotten away from him. He would usually be a few drinks deep by now, but he hadn't had a single drop.

Huh.

He noticed Monique's friends had left, and he expected Monique to approach him with some form of reprimand for giving away her secret identity. In fact, he'd been anticipating it all night. Why did he feel like he was about to get in trouble with the school principal?

If his punishment was anything like last time, he'd happily get punished again and again.

"I'll clean dishes for a week if you fess up about why Monique was so pissed off with you last week," Kyle teased while actually cleaning some glasses. He really wanted to know why Monique had been so desperate—and clearly infuriated—when asking Kyle for David's address last week. He'd tried a number of bribes up to this point to get him to spill.

But David remained tight-lipped.

"I'm not fessing up, bro. My lips are sealed."

"You know what? I give up. You win. And I must say, I'm impressed that she actually managed to shut up that blabbermouth of yours. I've been trying for years and failed miserably."

David slapped Kyle across the back of the head with a playful grin. "Whatever, man."

David could have sworn he'd seen Monique saying her goodbyes to her friends moments ago—but now she was gone. And with her disappearance, his resolve and work ethic for the evening dissipated into thin air.

Can I CU 2nite, David typed out with his thumbs on his Nokia while walking out of the bar and up the street. He didn't know if she was into text messaging. None of his friends responded to texts, but many of the ladies he got numbers from did—so it was worth a shot.

But instead of getting a message back, she called.

"You just saw me tonight, silly boy," she said in her sensually scolding way.

"I've been waiting patiently for my next punishment. I do deserve one, don't I?"

The silence and deep breathing on the other end of the line spoke volumes. He had her speechless. Tongue-tied.

Exactly where he wanted her.

"Punishment was on the cards, but now... praise may be more fitting. The whole situation, to my surprise, turned out far better than I expected. And I guess I should thank you for that."

"Well, that was my plan all along. To please you. So, can I come see you tonight?"

"I'm afraid I'm not at my house."

"Where are you?"

"I'm on your doorstep, waiting for you to get home and let me in."

Chapter 12

Monique

He had her in a chokehold. Not literally. Figuratively.

Well... maybe literally was on the table too.

Get your mind out of the gutter, girl.

She'd never been this hot and bothered by a man before. Never wanted someone this badly. Logic had been overridden by pure desire, leading her straight to David's doorstep. She hadn't even considered whether Kyle might be home. Awkward. But it looked like he was out—only David's car in the driveway, lights off.

Maybe she should go. This was a bad idea.

She stood from the stoop, brushing her hands down her skin-tight skirt— then she heard him.

"Come to tempt me again, Monique...?"

He let her name drag across his tongue like melted chocolate. Deep. Rough. Divine. That sound alone kept her rooted to the spot. But she had power over him, too. She knew it. Otherwise, he wouldn't be here.

"Like I said," she purred, stepping closer, "I'm here to dole out a mix of praise and punishment. And my methods? Tortuously slow."

David stepped closer "I'll take a lick, a bite, a twist—whatever's on your menu, baby. Bring it on."

He leaned in fast, stealing a kiss—quick and hungry. But her hand slid to the back of his head, her tongue coaxing him into something slower. Deeper. Torture by pleasure.

Oh, he was like a dog on heat. Eager. Desperate. Exactly where she wanted him.

She strutted into the house and toward the bedroom, hips swaying, David trailing behind, eyes locked on the view. When she turned, he was already a breath away, undoing his shirt one agonising button at a time.

Monique turned her back, letting her zipper slide down slowly—revealing bare skin, then the black thong beneath.

His hand grazed her ass.

She slapped it away.

Turning, she wagged a finger. "Na-ah-ah."

"You're the devil," David growled.

"And you're a rascal."

She peeled his shirt off, revealing sculpted abs and smooth skin. Her fingers traced feather-light paths over his chest, around his shoulders, until she pressed in for a long, drugging kiss. He lifted her off the ground, and gravity did the rest—her dress slipped to the floor, skin against skin.

The kiss grew hungrier. Her fingers twisted his nipples. He moaned, dropped her to the ground, and her tongue replaced her fingers—swirling, licking, teasing.

She kissed her way down, unbuckled his pants, and tugged them down slowly.

His cock stood proud, thick and ready.

"Fuck, Monique. I want you to taste me. Lick me."

"Ohhh, someone's impatient."

His hand wrapped in her hair, firm but restrained.

"Take me."

"Only if you say please."

Her lips hovered an inch away, breath hot against him. He could've forced her mouth onto him—but he didn't. He waited. For her.

Satisfied with his restraint, she took him in—slow, deep, deliberate. His moans grew ragged, his hips thrusting with abandon. Just when he was on the edge, she pulled back, leaving him slick and wanting.

"Now," she teased, "who wants to take a ride on my pony?"

David tipped an imaginary hat. "Yes, ma'am."

He crossed to the CD player with a smirk. "Now it's your turn to wait," he said, flipping through the discs until he found one and slid it in.

"Pony" by Ginuwine pulsed through the speakers.

Monique rolled her eyes, hands planted on her hips, as David strutted toward her with a ridiculous—yet undeniably sexy—giddy-up motion, one hand in the air, and the other smacking his bare backside like a one-man strip show. All confidence. No shame.

His face was stern, cock still rock hard, abs begging to be worshipped.

Yep. This was doing all kinds of things to her.

She danced for him, slow and sensual, in her lacy black bra and thong, desperate to get the upper hand in this game of seduction. Then he moved toward her, thrusting his hips in rhythm with the music, grinning wide.

Oh no. She was done for.

How did he make that look so damn hot?

He reached into the nearby drawer, pulled out a foil packet, and ripped it open. "Safety first, ma'am."

He backed her to the bed, towering over her. She slid onto the mattress as he hovered above, arms outstretched, eyes locked on hers. Waiting. Tempting. Trying to break her.

"So..." he said, voice dripping with seduction.

She clenched her thighs, aching. He wedged his knee between them, forcing them apart.

She needed him. On her. In her.

Before she could pull him down towards her, David growled, "Fuck it. You win."

In a heartbeat, he was on his knees, pulling her thighs toward him. He slid the G-string off completely, anchored his hands at her hips and entered her—slow, deep, devastating.

"David, I..." she gasped.

He leaned in, lips at her ear.

"Your apology has been accepted."

Then he slammed into her—hard, again, and again—kissing her neck, filling her completely.

She had no words. Only sensation. Only him.

"Fuck me," she whimpered, and he gripped the headboard with one hand, anchoring himself deeper.

His face strained, body slick with sweat. It was all she could see. All she wanted to see.

That thought, paired with the rhythm of his thrusts, sent her over the edge. Her moans were long, luscious, and loud. His followed—deep, guttural, melting into hers.

They collapsed together. Breathless. Spent.

The high was unlike anything she'd felt before. Just like the first time they did the dirty deed.

But as the haze faded, reality crept in.

That feeling—the way she looked at him when she came—scared her.

Looking at David's sweaty, naked body across the bed, something earth-shattering lingered.

Too big. Too real.

She couldn't handle it.

She needed to end this.

Whatever this was.

But she had no idea how.

Chapter 13

Monique

Monique woke up staring at an unfamiliar ceiling fan rattling at high speed above her, the early morning light casting strange shadows across its surface. That's right. She ended up at David's house. *Again.*

She *was* on her way to her place—or at least, that had been the intention before desire overrode logic. Her lips curved into a rueful smile. She was supposed to be cutting things off with David, not finding her way into his bed again. But last night, as she'd performed her set at the Cyder Lounge, her eyes had kept finding his across the dimly lit room. Her mother's voice had whispered warnings in her ear—*men just hold you back, sweetheart*—but her pulse had drowned out everything else.

While chatting with her newfound 'friends' last night—she figured she could call them that now, and she had him to thank for it—she couldn't help but sneak glances at David and admire how fine he looked. There had been something different about him, something she'd never seen before—a contentment, a settled ease that made the usual sharp edges of his personality seem softer, more approachable. It had driven her wild despite her mind screaming *no, steer clear, remember what Mum taught you.*

And now here she was, wrapped up in his black satin sheets, after a night of rough, wild sex that she was still riding the high of.

The raw magnetism between them was like a crack of thunder guaranteed to hit the ground and ignite. She couldn't control it, yet she was utterly consumed by it. By this bewitching man who smelled of LYNX Africa, Bundy rum and sweat, and looked like a male model straight out of a Bonds commercial. The intoxicating scent of him clung to her skin, marking her in ways that felt dangerously permanent.

She extricated herself from the tangled sheets and padded to the bathroom. In the mirror, her reflection told the story of last night's surrender—tousled hair, smudged mascara, lips still slightly swollen from his kisses. *What would Mum think of you now?* Her mother had raised her alone, fierce and independent, never needing a man's validation or support. *"Men are temporary, Monique,"* she'd say, *"but your dreams are forever."* Now here she was, risking her singing career—her actual dream—for what? A few hours of skin-on-skin with a man who'd made it clear from the start he wasn't the relationship type?

As if summoning him by pure thought alone, David waltzed in looking surprisingly refreshed and fully dressed, his dark hair still damp from a shower. Something in her chest tightened at the sight of him—casual confidence in worn jeans and a simple black t-shirt that hugged his shoulders in all the right ways.

"I need to show you something." His voice carried that familiar playful tone, but there was an undercurrent of something else—nervousness?

Since when did he call her Mon?

"I'm going to need at least an hour to sort this out first," Monique slurred out, gesturing to her face and undergarments strewn across his bedroom floor.

David leaned against the doorframe, one corner of his mouth lifting in that devastating half-smile that had first caught her attention months ago. "Now if I told you that this something involved the best coffee you've ever tasted in your life, would that shave a few minutes off that estimate?"

She tried to ignore the flutter in her stomach. This was dangerous territory—coffee dates were for couples, not whatever casual arrangement they'd fallen into. "Perhaps," she replied, forcing casualness into her voice, "but I'm not giving you any guarantees."

Forty-five minutes later, Monique found herself in the passenger seat of David's black Nissan Skyline, being driven through the sun-drenched streets of Brisbane. The leather seat was hot against her bare legs, and she shifted uncomfortably, tugging at the hem of last night's dress. *Where was he taking her?* For the whole ten-minute trip, she sat there listening to David talking about... himself.

But not in the usual way. Instead of boasting about conquests or deals at the Lounge, he spoke quietly about his childhood—about growing up with the larger-than-life presence of Samuel "Sammy" Sparks, the kind of father who filled every room with noise and charm and expectation.

"And how about your mum. Where is she?"

Silence. His expression stern. Reflective. And then, almost abruptly, the mood shifted.

"She just packed up one day," he said, knuckles whitening slightly on the steering wheel. "A few weeks before high school graduation. Ran off with another bloke. Dad and I haven't spoken to her since."

He hadn't seen his mother in...four years? That quiet shrug—so practiced, so hollow—spoke louder than any grief. Monique felt his pain like a punch to the gut.

The drinking. The shallow relationships. The untethered lifestyle all made more sense now.

It wasn't recklessness. It was fallout.

And suddenly, all the jagged pieces of him made sense.

But every piece of him he shared made her feel more and more unsettled. He shouldn't be sharing these things with her. What did he think this was? A relationship? The last thing she wanted was to be someone's rehabilitation project—the woman who taught David Sparks how to love again. That wasn't her. She was Monique Chambers, daughter of Catherine Chambers, who'd taught her that depending on *yourself* was the only way to ensure you weren't left behind.

The car slowed, and she looked up to see they'd arrived at an icon in Australian café franchises—the Coffee Club. She could smell the coffee beans roasting as soon as she stepped out of the car, the rich aroma mingling with the humid Brisbane air. The coffee must be good, she thought, noting the line stretching out the door. As expected, it was filled to the brim with people seeking weekend brunch and caffeine fixes.

As Monique wandered through the glass doors expecting to pick up a coffee to go, David led her over to a table with a reserved sign. Her heartbeat quickened uncomfortably.

"When did you reserve this?" she asked, her voice sharper than intended.

David rubbed the back of his neck, not quite meeting her eyes. "First thing this morning. This place is off the hook for a hangover feed. Let me go order. I'll be right back."

As he walked away, Monique watched him—the confident stride, the easy way he chatted with the barista. Several women in the café tracked his movement with appreciative glances. Why wouldn't they? David Sparks was the dictionary definition of a catch, if catching was what you were after. But Monique wasn't. She couldn't be.

She paid attention to the song playing softly over the café speakers— **"Most Girls" by Pink**—and found herself paying attention to the lyrics while tapping her foot incessantly under the table. When she forced it to stop, her fingers tapped at the table furiously instead. The rhythm matched the building panic in her chest.

Her mother's voice echoed in her mind: *"The moment you start depending on a man is the moment you start losing yourself."*

When he returned, she stood up to order for herself—to regain some control over this situation that was rapidly spiralling—but he told her to sit back down, his hand briefly touching her shoulder. The casual contact sent an unwelcome warmth through her.

"It's fine. I've got it," he said with a grin.

"What? You ordered for me?" She couldn't keep the edge from her voice.

"Yep." He nodded, sliding into the chair opposite. "That's the surprise."

Monique narrowed her eyes at him, desperately trying to see through this elaborate charade. The morning sunlight caught in his dark hair, highlighting those streaks of caramel that only appeared in certain light. Stop noticing these things, she chided herself.

"Seriously? Are you having a lend of me?"

David's brow furrowed. "What are you talking about?"

She leaned forward, lowering her voice. "Are you trying to play boyfriend and girlfriend here or something?"

David let out an overexaggerated 'Ha' of a laugh while slapping both palms on the table, drawing glances from nearby diners. "Mon. Really? We've talked about this. You know I'm not the kind of guy that gets tied down."

The words stung more than they should have. "Exactly," she said, picking up a sugar packet and folding it between her fingers. "That's why we shouldn't be here doing this."

"Come on, Monique, it's just one—"

"Date?" She cut him off, crushing the sugar packet. "Is that what this is? Because it sure looks like it. Barista-made coffee and brunch ordered and paid for by you. What else would you call it?"

David's jaw tightened, a flash of something—hurt?—crossing his features before being replaced by his usual easy smile. "It's just a post-bang breakfast. It doesn't mean anything."

"Doesn't it?" Her voice rose slightly before she caught herself. "Because it's beginning to feel like a lot more than whatever this is supposed to be. More than either of us wants it to be."

A waitress placed two cappuccinos onto the table in front of them, the foam art perfectly formed into delicate leaf patterns. The rich aroma wafted between them, temporarily breaking the sour mood that had fallen.

David opened his mouth, seemingly about to come up with another excuse for why he brought her on this non-date (which clearly was a date), when his face suddenly dropped. The fork he'd been fiddling with fell out of his hand and clanked loudly to the floor.

"Well, well, what do we have here?"

She didn't need to turn around to see him. Monique already knew that voice, as familiar to her as the microphone at the Lounge. It was Samuel Sparks. David's dad and her boss.

"Nice to see you, Monique," Samuel said as he stepped across to David's side of the table, his eyes casually glancing over her outfit, which was the exact same one she'd worn for her performance last night. Shit, shit, shit.

Monique was mortified. If she could crawl under the table and die, she would. Instead, on the surface, she remained composed. Controlled. As though everything about this situation was exactly as she willed it, despite it being so far from reality that she might as well be in the Matrix. Her heart pounded so loudly she was certain both men could hear it.

"Absolutely superb show you put on last night, darlin'," Sammy continued, his gaze shifting between her and his son. His voice carried its usual jovial tone, but there was steel underneath. "Now what you're doing out here with this schmuck I dunno, but I hope he's being a gentleman. You hear me, son?"

David made a spluttering cough sound into his napkin; his eyes fixed on the table.

"Now don't mind my rudeness, Monique, but I just want to steal this bloke away from you for a moment." Samuel's hand came down on David's shoulder, grip visibly tightening.

"Sure, ah, no problem." She managed to keep her voice steady, even as her stomach twisted into knots.

David stood from the table, flashing apologetic eyes at her before being led outside the café. If she moved her head slightly, she could just see them both talking tensely on the sidewalk. Samuel's gestures were animated, angry. David stood silent with his hand pressed hard to his forehead, occasionally running it through his hair in that way he did when stressed.

This was not good. This surely had something to do with them, with this situation they had fallen into. No, she couldn't blame him. Not entirely. She had wanted this too, had gone back time and again despite knowing better. But it had gone on too long, and they had gotten in too deep. Now that his dad knew—the man who signed her paychecks, who had given her the platform to pursue her singing dream—how could she ever face either of them at the club again?

She sat there, spiralling, pondering what to do. The cappuccino grew cold before her, the leaf design blurring into the darkening foam. Then a plate of food was placed in front of her by a smiling waitress. A folded wrap filled with bacon, egg, cheese, barbecue sauce and a hash brown. It was a breakfast burrito, and it was perfect. Exactly what she would have ordered for herself.

That was the nail in the coffin. He knew her—really knew her. And she was starting to know him too, beyond the cocky exterior and the playboy reputation. The thought terrified her more than any stage fright ever had.

She grabbed her purse and stood up just as David was making his way back inside, his expression unreadable. Their eyes met through the glass door, and something twisted in her chest—regret, longing, fear, she couldn't tell.

She was almost to the door when he intercepted her.

"Mon, where are you going? Come back." He reached for her arm but stopped short of touching her. She brushed past him and pushed through the door of the Coffee Club.

"I can't. I'm done." She said over her shoulder as David followed behind her. She looked up and down the street. Sammy was gone at least. That was a relief.

"What? Surely you don't mean that." His voice dropped, genuine concern replacing his usual bravado.

"Oh, but I do." She glanced back at the table through the coffee shop window—at the perfectly chosen breakfast and coffee getting cold. "This is beginning to look too much like a relationship to me, and unless you actually want me to be your girlfriend, I'm out."

Something flickered in his eyes—vulnerability quickly masked by his familiar defence mechanism. "Sounds to me like you want to be my girlfriend?" The teasing tone didn't quite reach his eyes.

"No, David." She shook her head slowly. "Like you said, you're not that kind of guy. You're far too immature to have one, obviously." The words came out harsher than intended, a shield against the dangerous softening she felt toward him.

"Ouch!" He pressed a hand to his chest in mock hurt, but she could see the real pain underneath. "Fine. You're right. Let's just pretend me shouting you breakfast didn't happen, and we can move on with our lives. Go back to the way things were. Deal?"

Going back would be so easy. And so dangerous.

"I can't do that, David."

"But why?" The facade dropped completely now, genuine confusion and hurt etched across his features.

She hated that he stood there, looking at her as if she'd just split the world in two. As if they ever had anything real worthy of losing in the first place. She'd never had anything real, not since losing her mum to cancer a year ago. And she knew she never would. Her mother's words echoed in her mind: *"To get what you want in life, sometimes you have to be a cold-hearted bitch."*

That meant she would always be alone. Because as soon as she let anyone too close, they somehow managed to threaten her dreams. David was the perfect example of that—his father's disapproving look had made it clear her position at the Lounge was now precarious at best.

"Because. I care too much." Her voice softened, the admission costing her. "And I shouldn't care this much. I can't care this much. Because we will never be anything to each other."

"Okay. I hear you." David swallowed hard, Adam's apple bobbing. "But... what about the Cyder Lounge?"

The question hung between them—her dream, the stage that had become home, the only place she felt her mother's presence still guiding her.

"I guess you can call this my resignation." Each word felt like swallowing glass. "I've got a real job. One where I was promoted. I'm making more than enough money now. I don't need to perform. Not anymore."

The lie tasted bitter. Her team leader job at the call centre paid the bills, but it would never feed her soul the way singing did. Her mother would be so disappointed with her. For giving up on this dream because of some man. And so she should be, because she was woefully disappointed in herself too.

"Yes, you do." David's voice grew intense, his eyes locking with hers. "That's what you do. That's your *thing*. You're too good at it to stop."

For a moment, she allowed herself to hear the admiration in his voice—genuine appreciation for her talent, not just her body.

"That means a lot," she whispered, "but it's not enough."

"Nope, I can't accept that. I won't." He stepped closer, close enough that she could smell that damned LYNX Africa again. "Look, I know you're pissed with me for buying you breakfast. I get it. My chivalry got the better of me. But if you won't stay for me, do it for Sammy. Do it for the club. We need you."

That was the only argument right now that could sway her. Her mother's voice again: *"Never let a man come between you and your dreams."* But Monique knew that if she stayed at the Cyder Lounge, she'd keep being reeled back to him. Every night on that stage, seeing him at the bar, knowing what those hands felt like on her skin... She needed a clean break, and he needed it too, even if he couldn't accept that right now. It was the only way they could end this for good.

"You'll have to," she said finally, forcing strength into her voice. She reached up, briefly touching his cheek—a goodbye. "This is my choice, and you need to accept that. I'm sorry. Please apologise to Sammy for me."

As she walked away, the Brisbane sun hot on her bare shoulders, she thought she heard him call her name once more. She didn't turn around. Her mother had taught her that walking away was sometimes the hardest part of being strong. What her mother hadn't taught her was how much it could hurt to be strong in exactly the way she'd been raised to be.

Chapter 14

David

David's keys clattered against the hallway table as he stumbled through the front door, the takeaway container from the Coffee Club growing heavier in his grip with each step. The house felt like a tomb—too quiet, too empty, too much space for his thoughts to echo around in.

"Well, well, look what the cat dragged in." Kyle's voice drifted from the lounge room, dripping with smugness. "How'd the breakfast go, Romeo?"

David didn't answer. He went straight to the kitchen. He needed a drink. It was barely noon, but the Bundy rum on the top shelf called like an old friend.

Kyle wandered in from the lounge, sipping coffee and crunching cereal from a chipped bowl. He'd come home a few hours earlier, some story about spending the night with a girl. David felt Kyle's judgement settle like a weight when he realised Monique had stayed over *and* he watched them head out together to get breakfast.

"That bad, eh?" Kyle appeared in the doorway, cradling a coffee and wearing that infuriating I-told-you-so expression David had been dreading. "Mate. What did you think was gonna happen?"

"Piss off, Kyle." David's hand shook slightly as he poured three fingers of rum into a Big Day Out stubby holder. *Only* a stubby holder. Nope. No cup inside. Shit. He threw it down his throat fast. The amber liquid burned, but not nearly enough to numb how pissed off he felt about the whole situation.

"Mate, I warned you about this." Kyle settled against the bench, clearly settling in for a proper lecture. "Remember? 'Don't shit where you eat,' but no, you had to go and catch feelings for the talent."

David took another swig, larger this time. The radio in the background droned on about Y2K preparations—some expert warning that Australian banks might not be ready for the millennium rollover, that cash machines could fail, that people should stock up on tinned food and bottled water. The whole world was preparing for disaster, and here he was, having just created his own personal apocalypse. But Kyle was wrong. He hadn't caught any feelings. He was incapable of it.

"You know what your problem is?" Kyle continued, apparently taking David's silence as encouragement. "You think you're some kind of leading man. Taking what you want with no repercussions and a guaranteed happy ending despite the costs along the way."

"She called me immature." The words slipped out before David could stop them.

Kyle nearly choked on his cereal. "Immature? You? Never would've guessed." He gestured at the rum bottle. "What time is it again? Oh right, it's not even midday and look at you."

David's Nokia sat on the counter like an accusation. He'd tried calling her twice on the drive home—straight to Message Bank both times. Her voice, cool and professional: "You've reached Monique. Leave a message." He hadn't.

"The old man cornered us at the café," David said, staring into his drink. "Saw us together. Knew exactly what was going on."

"Sammy Sparks caught you? Christ, mate." Kyle's smugness faltered for a moment. "No wonder she ran. You've probably cost her the gig."

That hit harder than David expected. Monique loved that stage more than anything—and now, because of their stupid arrangement, because he couldn't keep his hands to himself, she lost that too. Sammy didn't want her gone; David was the one under fire for endangering the act and the patrons. Dad had been right. He'd blown it.

The radio commentary switched to a song. **"I Want It That Way" by The**

Backstreet Boys. Cringey as the boy-band song was, the lyrics landed harder than they should have. Because he wasn't heartbroken. Just disappointed things had to end on such a sour note when he thought he was doing something nice and selfless for once. A lot of good *that* did him.

"You know what you need?" Kyle said, rinsing his bowl in the sink. "A reality check. She was always going to walk away from whatever was going on between you two eventually. Chicks like that—they're career-focused. They don't stick around for blokes like—"

"Me? That's what you were going to say wasn't it? What's that supposed to mean?"

"Oh, come off it. You work at your dad's pub; you drive a Skyline. You can barely afford the payments on, and your biggest achievement this year was talking that backpacker from Sweden into a threesome with her mate." Kyle's words cut deep because they held uncomfortable truth. "Meanwhile, she's got that fancy job, she's got talent, she's going places. What did you think was going to happen?"

David wanted to argue, to list all the reasons Kyle was wrong. But the takeaway container sat there on the bench like evidence against him.

The song faded out, and the Y2K expert on the radio was back and getting more dramatic: "...complete system failure is a real possibility. We could be looking at a return to the dark ages, folks. Cash only transactions, no electronic records..."

"Maybe that wouldn't be so bad," David muttered.

"What, the apocalypse?" Kyle popped two pieces of bread in the toaster. "Mate, you're really losing it if you think the end of the world would solve your problems."

But David was thinking about Monique's words: "I can't care this much." As if caring was a weakness, a failing on her part. Maybe she was right. Maybe caring was the problem. He'd spent months telling himself their arrangement was perfect—no strings, no complications, just attraction and great sex. When had it become something else? When had he started staying the night and ordering her breakfast?

David's phone buzzed. For a split second, his heart leaped, but it was just a text from his father: "Need to talk. Come in early tonight."

"See? Already moving on to the next drama." Kyle peered at the message over David's shoulder. "Probably wants to discuss the Monique situation. Bet he's ropeable."

The thought of facing his father's disappointment made David reach for the rum bottle again. Samuel Sparks had built the Cyder Lounge from nothing, and David had just potentially cost him his best performer. The golden child had well and truly tarnished.

"You know what?" David straightened, liquid courage warming his voice. "Stuff this moping-around bullshit. It's nearly the year 2000—we're about to hit a new millennium. It's her loss. There are more fish in the sea than I'll ever need. Maybe she was right. What we had was dragging on. Time to cut the tie."

Kyle's grin widened as he smeared Vegemite on his toast. "Good thing she already did that for you. Let her drift out to sea until she's too far to catch. Best for both of you, before feelings get involved, right?"

David nodded, but his eyes drifted to the takeaway container again. He could picture Monique's face when she realised what he'd ordered—the brief softening before she caught herself, before the walls went back up.

"David?" Kyle waved a hand in front of his face. "You still with me?"

"Yeah." David shook his head, dispelling the image. "Yeah, you're absolutely right. Time to get back to basics."

He picked up the container and dumped it in the bin, breakfast burrito and all. If Monique wanted to walk away and disappear from his life like she never existed, he could play that game too. In fact, he'd play it better than anyone.

Chapter 15

Monique

Through the thin glass wall that sealed her status and separated her from her team, she could see the call centre floor buzzing with desperate energy—her team trying to meet impossible quotas while the world outside prepared for a potential digital apocalypse as they approached the dawn of a new millennium.

A soft knock interrupted her thoughts. Julie appeared in the doorway, perfectly manicured nails tapping against the door frame.

"A certain someone is on her way to see you." Julie's smile was bright, despite the ominous news she was sharing.

"Wonderful." Monique didn't look up from her reports despite her heart thundering beneath her chest, maintaining the professional distance she'd cultivated since her promotion to team leader.

"Just thought you should know, she looks pissed off too." Julie stepped inside and closed the door—of course she did. Always had to be a witness whenever any office drama popped up, and Monique had a feeling she would be at the centre of it this time.

Monique's pen stilled on the page. "I have no idea why." Of course she knew why. Her focus and drive at work had faded to nothing ever since she cut ties with David and the Cyder Lounge. David and that place had etched themselves so deeply into her that it felt like a part of her had been carved out and lost forever. No matter how hard she tried, she couldn't tear her mind away from that truth. She thought staying busy—managing her team, hitting quotas—might help. Might distract her long enough to move on. But the work only echoed what was missing. Each task reminded her of what she'd lost, and the drive that once fuelled her performance slowly withered into nothing. She didn't know how to get it back. Or if she even could.

"I appreciate you coming to warn me," Monique said carefully, finally meeting Julie's gaze. Thank God for Julie. She was one of the first people Monique felt safe enough to lower her walls around in this place. After everything she'd been dealing with lately, it was a relief to have someone who listened. She'd never had that before. Not since her mum died. Her mother had been her only friend, her fiercest supporter, and no one had ever come close to filling that space. But Julie was someone she could call a friend. And somehow, that helped ease the ache. Just a little.

"So...have you heard from David?" Julie asked.

The sound of his name stung more than it should have, sending sharp shots of pain and disappointment to her brain. Julie was the only person who knew about the fling with David that cost Monique the Cyder Lounge gig, the only one Monique had trusted with that secret. But before Monique could respond, Janice's heavy footsteps echoed down the corridor. Their manager moved through the call centre like a battleship cutting through choppy waters, her severe grey suit and tightly pulled-back hair giving her an intimidating presence.

"Chambers." Janice appeared in the doorway, her voice cutting through the air like glass. "We need to discuss your team's performance. Now."

Julie didn't even try to leave. If anything, she shrank deeper into the corner, hoping the towering inferno of a woman wouldn't notice her at all.

Janice shot Julie a disinterested glance, then fixed her steely gaze on Monique. "Your team's completion rates are down fifteen percent this week. Henderson's unit is outperforming yours by a significant margin."

Monique straightened in her chair, channelling the same cold profession-alism that had earned her this office in the first place. The corporate version of herself she'd been building like armour.

"The Y2K panic must have people on edge. They're hanging up faster than usual—"

"Everyone's dealing with Y2K anxiety," Barbara cut her off. "Yet Henderson's numbers are up. What does that tell you about leadership?"

The comparison stung, especially with Julie sitting right there taking it all in. Monique forced her expression to remain neutral, even as her mind couldn't shake the irony—here she was, being criticised for team management when just weeks ago she'd commanded a room full of people with nothing but her voice and presence.

"I understand your concern," Monique replied, her voice taking on the clipped, emotionless tone she'd perfected. "What do you need from me to improve team performance?"

Janice's eyes narrowed slightly, as if surprised by the lack of defensiveness. "I need you to remember that team leaders set the tone. If you're not fully committed to this role, it shows."

Monique felt a sprinkle of shame as Janice and Julie's eyes bore into her, waiting for any crack in the professional facade. "Of course. I'll implement new strategies immediately."

"Good," Janice said, her intimidating presence filling the small office. "I expect to see improvement by Friday. We can't afford distractions right now, not with all this millennium bug nonsense making people paranoid."

As Janice left, her footsteps echoing down the corridor, Julie lingered in the doorway.

"Brutal," Julie said with a pained expression. "Must be tough. This job I mean. Lots of pressure."

Monique caught sight of her reflection in the window nearby—sharp suit, severe expression, all traces of the sultry singer from the Cyder Lounge carefully erased. Her mother's voice whispered in her memory: *"Sometimes you have to be cold and keep to yourself to get what you want."*

Was this what her mother had meant? Was becoming like Janice—intimidating, ruthless, successful—the price of survival?

"I *am* worthy," Monique replied curtly, more so to herself than for Julie's ears. To validate herself out loud. Because she needed this job. Although one of her dreams may have slipped through her fingers, this job would get her the savings she needed to make the other dream real—to travel the world.

Julie gave a thin, strained smile—one that never reached her eyes—then slipped out the door. That berating from Janice swiftly reminded Monique of how precarious her position really was. She needed to pick up her game.

Alone in her office now, Monique turned back to her computer screen but found herself staring without seeing. She was becoming exactly like the people she'd once pitied—corporate drones who'd forgotten what it felt like to feel. To care.

Desperate to shake that feeling off, Monique hummed **"Steal My Sunshine" by LEN** softly to herself as she entered data into a spreadsheet on her computer. The act of singing, if only for herself, swiftly rekindled some hope and sense of self back into her bones.

As evening approached and the call centre cubicles began to empty, Monique gathered her reports and found herself singing now. Loud and proud. While walking to her car through the near-empty parking garage, she allowed the chorus to pass through her lips, her voice echoing softly off the concrete walls.

For just a moment, she sounded like herself again.

Chapter 16

David

New Year's Eve. A night David had eagerly anticipated in years past, but this year, the thrill of revelling in euphoric celebration and mayhem left a bitter taste in his mouth. It took more grog than usual to wash it away.

Nearing midnight, he headed for The Pulse nightclub. He'd lost the boys somewhere along the strip while weaving at speed through the crowd, but he didn't care. He played a better game on his own anyway—and he needed to find his next fix.

Once inside—**"Boom, Boom, Boom, Boom!" by the Vengaboys** blaring so loud he could barely hear himself think—David scanned the dance floor with mechanical precision, eyes darting past the crowd in search of a distraction.

The pulsing lights and thundering music did little to drown out the echo of Monique's parting words from weeks before: "You're just not mature enough," she'd said. The memory stung like acid.

Then he saw her.

Young. Probably fresh out of high school. Wide-eyed and glowing with that unmistakable mix of wonder and vulnerability, like everything around her was brand new.

Perfect.

Just the ego boost he needed.

Approaching her was almost too easy. A tap on her shoulder, a practised smile—and he watched her resolve melt instantly. They always did. The way she looked at him—like he was some kind of Prince Charming—sent a familiar rush of power through his veins.

As they danced, he pulled out all his usual moves: the confident grip, the slow sway, the intense eye contact that never failed. Her friend at the bar shot them a glance before wandering off.

Good. No interference.

He could feel her tension, her inexperience in every movement—the slight tremor in her fingers when he held her hand, the way she second-guessed each step. It was almost laughable how different she was from Monique's sophisticated confidence. But right now, that was exactly what he wanted.

"Want to grab a drink and chat?" he murmured, knowing full well how his voice affected women like her. "Get to know each other a little better?" The hesitation in her eyes lasted only a moment before she nodded.

They always did.

He led her to a secluded corner, maintaining his carefully crafted persona. "What's your name, gorgeous?" He watched her stammer out "Sarah" with satisfaction. Such a sweet, innocent name—so unlike Monique's exotic sophistication.

"Well, Sarah, you can just call me your Prince Charming. Or David, I suppose." He delivered the line with practised charm, watching it land exactly as intended. Her giggle was almost painfully naïve.

As the New Year's countdown began, he knew exactly how to play the moment. The timing was perfect—the excitement, the atmosphere, all working in his favour. "Here's to new beginnings," he said, though in his mind he was thinking only of endings—specifically, his ending with Monique.

He kissed her with well-practised expertise, noting with satisfaction how completely she melted into it. This was exactly what he needed: someone who would look at him with that starstruck expression, someone who would make him feel powerful again.

"Wow..." he rasped, playing up the affected awe while calculating his next move. As he traced his fingers along her frame, he could practically read her thoughts written across her face.

So young. So trusting. So eager to believe in romance.

"You're just so damn irresistible," he whispered, recycling the same line he'd used countless times before. "I can't help but want to hold you... touch you..."

Her whispered confession—about never meeting anyone like him before—almost made him laugh. If she only knew how many times he'd played this exact scene before. But she didn't need to know that. She just needed to help him forget Monique, if only for a little while.

After that kiss, he knew he would be going further with her than she had ever been with anyone—and that thought alone was exhilarating. Most women he'd slept with up to this point were seasoned, mature in the bedroom. It was not their first rodeo, and he'd learned a lot about the art of pleasuring a woman thanks to them.

But to capture the interest of Sarah—so young and naïve—almost felt sinister. As if taking her virginity for his pleasure were akin to crushing a delicate petal that could never be mended.

Guiding her through the motions, knowing that those little moans and the exposure of her naked body were witnessed for the first time by him—of all people—should have felt sacred. It should have been a treasured experience for someone more worthy, more devotional, more genuine.

But David was none of those things.

He was selfish. Craving. Hungry. Fuelled by the high of it—knowing he had won her affection. Won her virginity over all others in that nightclub.

But as she looked up at him with loved-up eyes, filled with unwarranted admiration, care, and kindness—paired with delicate caresses of her soft skin across his arms and chest, the way someone might stroke a treasured gift—his gut hollowed out.

Whatever this was, whatever they had done together, clearly meant so much more to her than it did to him.

And then, after it was done, and his sweat-covered body rolled off hers with heaving breaths of ecstasy, she said the words that would doom him.

"I think I love you."

Floored. Absolutely floored.

He felt sick. Horrendous. Guilty. Guilty for what he had done—despite her appearing entirely satisfied. Sexually, at least. In fact, more than satisfied.

She said she loved him.

How could he respond to that without breaking her fragile little heart?

So, somehow, he croaked out:

"You too…"

Now, if he had been doomed before, he absolutely was now.

What did he just say?

Lying in her bed, wrapped in her sheets, and now she was wrapping her hand in his—as if she were his and only his.

Oh no. This was bad. Very, very bad.

This was why he didn't sleep with women younger than him. They get attached. They don't want to let go.

But as he looked across at her face, flushed with joy, and felt the warm tug of her tightly gripped hand—perhaps he wouldn't let go either.

Well, not yet anyway.

The year 2000 hadn't ended the world, but he feared it would end hers.

It felt inevitable—and with his tendency to get bored and move on to the next distraction, he would be the reason why.

"I have a girlfriend," David said, not quite meeting Kyle's eyes.

"You have a girlfriend?"

"It appears so."

"But I thought you didn't do relationships."

"I kinda fell into one."

"Okay. Spill."

David had been sitting on this secret for three days, and he was nearly bursting at the seams to tell someone—anyone. Kyle would do. They were slouched on the couch, eating tinned spaghetti jaffles and flicking through the five channels on the TV, desperately searching for something decent to watch. The moment felt low-stakes enough to drop a bomb.

"I met this chick on New Year's Eve. She said she loved me, and I may have said something of that sort back."

Kyle sat forward, elbows pressed to his knees. "No..."

"Wait, it gets better. I left some of my shit at her house, and when I came back the next day to pick it up, she introduced me to her housemate Lauren as her boyfriend—and I kinda just went with it."

Kyle shook his head, digesting his jaffle as the phrase "The Price Is Right" rang out from the TV behind him. The sound finally made him put down the remote, ending his endless channel rotation.

"What the actual fuck. So, are you breaking your non-relationship off with her then?"

"What? No! Why would I do that?"

"Because you don't want to be in a relationship with her. Obviously."

"She doesn't need to know that."

"Um, yes she does—unless you plan on being loyal to her, which I know you won't be."

David sat in silence, dipping the corner of his jaffle into a squirt of barbecue sauce on his plate while watching a bunch of people on TV get far too excited about guessing the price of a home stereo system that played three CDs at a time.

"I don't want to hurt her."

"So break it off. You'll be hurting her more if you keep dragging this out."

"But I... I need this, man. Some stability, you know? Something real."

"As in a relationship? If that's what you want, you need to be all in—or it's nothing."

"I knew I shouldn't have told you."

"What did you expect me to say? 'Great job fucking over another girl'? Except now you've levelled up to emotionally fucking someone over instead of just physically fucking them."

"Fuck you, man. I do what I want. You don't understand."

Kyle shook his head, disgust written across his face.

"I do understand. I've been here this whole time, remember? It seems you might've forgotten—too caught up in your extracurricular lifestyle with those hang-offs you call friends. Just... stop victim-blaming, man. I get it. You have mummy issues. Don't take it out on other women. Or if you do, don't tell me about it unless you want me to put you in your place."

Why did he keep telling Kyle everything? Perhaps because he always had—even when he outright distanced himself from him in other areas of his life. Maybe, deep down, he wanted Kyle's judgment. He wanted to feel the full force of it because he knew he deserved it. Not just for what he was doing to Sarah, but for all the times he'd pushed Kyle away from his newfound social circles and social life.

He knew Kyle didn't deserve it. But that's the person David had formed himself into—someone who chased a good time at the expense of everyone around him. He couldn't change that. In fact, he had every intention of embracing it and drawing power from it.

They sat watching the rest of The Price Is Right in stony silence, eyes fixed on the screen, avoiding each other. A bloke named Leon was playing Cliffhanger—the game where a little paper mountain climber is pushed up a slope toward the edge of a cliff every time the player guesses a product's price wrong.

But every contestant took the risk. They had to. Because if their little sacrificial climber didn't fall off the edge, they'd win a prize—and the glory of that win would be broadcast live across Australia.

Leon's guesses kept missing the mark. One by one, they nudged the climber closer to doom. The shampoo pack did him in. Just three dollars off, and over the edge he went. No prize. No glory.

At least he got to meet Larry Emdur.

David wondered how long he could keep pushing this fake relationship along before hitting his own inevitable cliff—dragging them both over the edge.

Chapter 17

David

It was a warm Saturday afternoon, and somehow, David had found himself in a relationship with Sarah for two months. Fifty-six days, to be exact. How did that happen?

Today, he was having one of those days where he had to be somewhere else. Anywhere other than his place or his work. And "somewhere" ended up being right back at Sarah's front door.

This was how he'd ended up stuck in a relationship he never wanted. Kyle and Sammy were always pissed off at him about something, so he stopped seeking them out and lingering at the places they resided. Sarah was easy drop-in access to a bit of company and a good time—something he returned to over and over again out of convenience.

Before he had a chance to knock, the door swung open and Lauren—Sarah's gloomy best friend and housemate—appeared with a look of uninterested displeasure buried under eyes rimmed with so much eyeliner she looked like she'd just walked off the set of *Rage* at 2 a.m.

Before he could get a word out, Lauren spat one short, sharp word: "No." Then slammed the door in his face.

She did not like him. Since he'd started seeing Sarah, their run-ins had been frequent—and her attitude swung wildly between bored disinterest and outright hostility, especially when Sarah wasn't watching.

He'd taken a soccer ball to the groin, been "accidentally" singed on the arm by a lighter when Lauren tried to light a nearby candle, and tripped over a suspiciously placed black satchel bag covered in band pins right outside Sarah's bedroom.

All accidents, apparently. At least, that's what Lauren claimed. But he knew better.

"Who was that?" He could hear Sarah's voice murmur from behind the door.

The door swung open again, and this time he was greeted by Sarah's smiling face, with the song **"Every Morning" by Sugar Ray** playing clearly from somewhere inside the house—the lyrics echoing with an honesty he didn't want to admit.

She exuded even more joy than the night he met her, and he desperately wanted to soak some of it in. Bathe in it.

"Oh wow. Hello. Hi! Um... well, isn't this a lovely surprise!"

"Hey beautiful. I missed you. Really wanted to see your face again, girl. Hope I'm not intruding."

Then he noticed the orange Video Ezy shirt she was wearing.

"Oh, you're heading to work?"

"Yeah, about to catch the bus."

"Well, let me drop you off. It would be my pleasure."

As they talked in the car, their conversation felt robotic. Rehearsed. As if they were saying stock-standard lines from someone else's performance.

"How was your day?"

"Fine, thanks, how was yours?"

"What did you have for breakfast?"

It was empty. Surface-level. No depth.

But it was a distraction from the familiar, toxic world full of too many bad memories. And here, with Sarah, he found a life completely cut off from the one he knew—and this time, he'd keep it that way. She was too delicate and pure for his world, so he decided to protect her from it entirely. For her own good. And his.

"You know what tomorrow is, right?"

Sarah asked meekly.

"No. Sorry. You'll have to remind me."

"It's my first day at university. Remember? You said you'd come along and see me off."

Did he? Perhaps he'd said it in passing, hoping she'd forget. He had no interest in being seen in a place filled with wanky, educated elitists. No thank you. Not his scene at all.

"I'm so sorry, babe. I'm... busy."

She smiled and said it was okay, but he could see the disappointment in her eyes.

As Sarah waved at him through the window of his black Nissan Skyline, beaming from ear to ear as she walked into the Video Ezy store, he couldn't stop his mind from drifting to Monique.

The way she waved. The way she walked. The way she talked.

And he felt like the biggest dickhead in the world for it.

The campus was buzzing, students pouring out of lecture halls like ants from a cracked nest. David hadn't planned to be here—he'd popped by last minute. Guilt had gotten the better of him. And Kyle's relentless berating about what a dickhead he'd be if he didn't go might've had something to do with it too.

David stood just outside the crowd, scanning faces until he spotted her—Sarah, animated and glowing, chatting with some guy. He didn't recognise him, but the way the guy looked at her made David's chest tighten. Not jealousy, exactly. More like irritation. He wasn't in the mood to play boyfriend today, but he'd promised he'd show up.

She saw him and lit up like a Christmas tree.

"Oh my god, he actually came!"

Before he could brace himself, she was in his arms, all warmth and enthusiasm. David hugged her back, letting the moment play out. She was sweet. Too sweet. And she cared way more than he did—which made everything feel heavier than it should.

"It took me forever to find your lecture theatre," he said, throwing in a dramatic sigh for effect. "This university is a maze! Hope you appreciate me going out of my way to come see you."

He knew the tone he was taking. It was deliberate. Biting. Like he was above all this. But it was just a flimsy attempt to hide the shame and lack of care he felt for her.

"Oh, I do. I really, really do," she said, kissing him like he was the centre of her universe.

He kissed her back, but his eyes drifted to the guy she'd been talking to—awkward posture, nervous energy. David clocked him instantly.

"So, who's this?" he asked, letting a bit of edge creep into his voice.

"This is Michael; he's the first friend I've made here."

David wrapped an arm around Sarah's shoulders, more out of habit than feeling.

"I see. As long as it's nothing more than friends, you hear me, buddy?"

Sarah groaned.

"Oh, David, don't be like that. Not every guy is trying to get into my pants, you know?"

Michael combusted in real time, stammering through a trainwreck of words about pants and not liking pants and wearing pants. David raised an eyebrow, unimpressed.

"Okay… you are one strange dude."

Sarah smoothed it over, like she always did.

"Don't mind him, Michael. I'll see you at the rally later this week?"

Michael nodded, clearly still recovering, and David watched him linger a little too long as they walked away. He didn't like it. Not because he was threatened—he wasn't—but because it reminded him that Sarah was all in. And he wasn't.

She was still smiling, like she'd won some prize. Two months in and she was already imagining forever. David could feel it in the way she looked at him, like he was the answer to something.

But he hadn't signed up to be anyone's answer.

"So, how would you like to spend the rest of the afternoon?" she asked, hopeful. "A romantic stroll through the park? A movie?"

He winced internally. She meant well, but he had plans.

"Ah, sorry babe, I'm actually just dropping by on my way to meet up with some mates in the city."

Sarah blinked.

"Oh. Well. Can I come? I haven't met your friends yet."

He gave her the look—soft, apologetic, but firm.

"You won't like it. Just some guy stuff—beers, chilling. You don't mind, do you babe?"

She hesitated.

"No, I guess not."

David kissed her forehead, trying to smooth the disappointment.

"Don't worry, I'll make it up to you. I'll take you out to dinner one night and spoil you rotten. How does that sound?"

She didn't buy it. He could see it in her eyes.

"You told me that last week, David. And the week before. But you still haven't taken me out on a date."

"I will, I promise," he said, defaulting to charm. "You know I love you!"

She said it back, but it landed flat. He felt it. She was starting to notice the cracks.

Jogging toward the bus, David shoved his hands in his pockets and tried to ignore the gnawing guilt as a student blasted **"Lovefool" by the Cardigans** from a parked car, the lyrics pulling him into an unwanted reflection.

He hadn't meant to fall into this relationship. Sarah was lovely, but she wanted things he wasn't ready to give. Not yet. Maybe not ever.

Behind him, she was probably walking home alone, wondering why it didn't feel quite right.

He didn't have the answer.

He just knew he wasn't ready to be the guy she needed.

Because he desperately needed someone else.

Monique

The bass pulsed through Empire nightclub as Monique scanned the room, trying to look more comfortable than she felt. The new year had passed in a blur—how was it already March? She hadn't celebrated it. Barely wanted to acknowledge it.

But she was determined to follow through on one resolution—one Julie had set for her: to get out more. To party with her. To live a little.

The fact that David regularly haunted these places with his obnoxious entourage had nothing to do with it. And she was grateful he'd finally stopped the incessant texts and phone calls after New Year's. It made it easier to keep him out of her mind entirely.

But two months of forcing herself into these scenes, and these clubs still didn't quite feel like home. Not like the dimly lit stage at the Cyder Lounge had.

"I believe this is yours," the bartender said, handing her a glass of white wine.

Another new habit, courtesy of Julie and her party-going lifestyle. Monique understood now how people got hooked on the stuff—the way it softened the edges, made everything feel just a little more manageable.

She hadn't touched a drop since high school, when she got drunk playing goon of fortune, made a complete fool of herself, blacked out in a wheelie bin, and swore she'd never drink again.

But these days, she craved something to take the edge off. Just a little.

"You're not still thinking about him, are you?" Julie nudged her elbow. "Because if you are, please stop."

After the fallout with David last year, Monique couldn't hold it all in. She had to tell someone—so the churning emotions within her didn't eat her from the inside out. And Julie was more than happy to gobble up the gory details of their passionate fling.

"I'm not," Monique lied, adjusting the strap of her velvet dress. She'd chosen the dark red number deliberately tonight—confidence armour. She needed it after the week she'd had, dealing with frustrated customers and training new hires. Being a call centre team leader in the year 2000 meant constant stress over new systems and millennium bug fallout that still affected some of their clients.

"Good, because men like that—" Julie stopped mid-sentence, her eyes widening as she stared over Monique's shoulder.

"Speaking of the devil... Don't look now, but guess who just walked in."

Monique's heart skipped. She didn't need to turn around. The energy in the room had shifted—the way it always did when David entered a space. Like he owned it. Like everyone should notice.

She took a long, deliberate sip of her drink, steeling herself.

"Is he looking this way?"

"He's spotted you. And yes, he's coming over with his entourage. God, they look half-cut already."

"Smooth" by Santana and Rob Thomas played over the nightclub speakers as Monique straightened her spine, preparing for battle. Three months of passion and pain coursed through her memory—the way his eyes had lit up the first time she performed at his father's bar, how quickly he'd charmed his way into her life, her bed. How she gave up the last shred of something she genuinely enjoyed to avoid him. And here he was, strolling back into her life like he'd never left.

"I'm not interested," she said, mostly to convince herself.

"Your face says otherwise," Julie muttered.

And then he was there, standing before her with that infuriating confidence, flexing those shoulders she had once traced with her fingertips. The familiar scent of Lynx Africa hit her senses before his ridiculous line did.

"Hey beautiful, you're looking as gorgeous as ever. If beauty was a drop of water, you'd be the entire ocean."

She fought the urge to laugh—or worse, smile. Instead, she rolled her eyes, feigning annoyance while her pulse betrayed her.

"Well, well, if it isn't Mr Ladies' Man himself. I'm surprised they even let you through the door after getting kicked out of here twice before."

She watched satisfaction flash across his face. Yes, she remembered. She remembered everything, which was the problem.

"Don't be like that, baby," he said, leaning closer, his voice dropping to that intimate tone that used to make her melt.

"You know you're the only one for me. Don't you remember how incredible we were together? We set the world on fire. Let's reignite that magic."

Yep. He was absolutely sloshed. What was this utter trash coming out of his mouth? He was laying on the cheesy lines thick tonight. It almost seemed like he was putting on a show for the boys.

The song changed to **"Don't Call Me Baby" by Madison Avenue**, and Monique felt something shift inside her—a desire to take control of this narrative for once. If David wanted to put on a show, she'd give him one.

She stood, grabbed his hand, and pulled him onto the dancefloor. Her body moved against his, remembering how to tease and tantalise without giving in. Each sway of her hips was calculated warfare, each brush of her body against his a reminder of what he'd thrown away.

His friends watched from across the room, clearly expecting David to work his usual charm. But Monique was done being another conquest. As she sang along to the lyrics, she injected every word with the fury and desire that had been simmering inside her for months.

She backed him into a corner, gratified to see him flustered for once, uncertain of his next move. When she pushed him down into a chair, the power shift was palpable.

Towering over him, she leaned in close enough to smell the UDL on his breath.

"Don't come near me," she warned, her voice low and dangerous.

"I don't want to see your face again."

The lie tasted bitter on her tongue, but the look on his face—confusion, arousal, frustration—made it worthwhile. She turned away before he could see the conflict in her eyes, rejoining her friend.

"We're leaving," she announced, grabbing her purse.

Monique allowed herself one last glance over her shoulder. David sat where she'd left him, watching her go, his friends already laughing at his expense.

Good. Let him feel a fraction of the humiliation she'd felt.

Monique pushed through the exit doors into the cool night air. But as the club music faded behind them, she couldn't ignore the heat still coursing through her veins—or the certainty that this wasn't the end of their story.

Not by a long shot.

Chapter 18

David

Hitting the gym and pounding the treadmill forced David to think. Really think. About last night, as he listened to **"Man of The Hour" by John Farnham** on his Discman.

Sure, he was tanked, but that was no excuse for how hard he'd failed with Monique. And was she drinking wine? Since when did she drink? He was going to call her. Needed to get a few things straight. She probably wouldn't pick up—like every other time before—but it was worth a shot.

One ring. Two. Three...

"Hello?" Monique's velvet voice filtered through the phone.

Before he had a chance to respond, her voice boomed through the tiny Nokia speaker.

"What was up with that cocky display you put on last night? I'm surprised you'd even try to call me after that embarrassing performance."

"What do you mean? I was simply my usual charming self."

"No. What you put on was a show. It seemed like you were trying to impress your friends, but for some reason, they didn't appear to be taken by your tactics. I wonder why?"

Ooh, she was sassy. And mad. And even though Monique was clearly paying him out, he couldn't help but grin from ear to ear.

"I don't know what you're talking about. I'm a legend—my boys love me."

Monique sucked in a deep breath before sighing heavily on the other end of the line.

"You're nothing but a scared and hurt little boy, trying desperately to fill some kind of void you refuse to acknowledge. And your 'boys' don't love you. They loathe you. They only put up with you so they can use you for a free night out."

That was far too heavy for him to process at this time of morning. Who was she—his psychiatrist?

"You're just jealous that I have friends."

"Goodbye, David."

The engaged signal rang out.

Yep. He deserved that. Running his stupid mouth again, hitting her where it hurt just to make himself feel better. But it wasn't game over. Monique was a catch he couldn't let slip away. He'd already let her go once, but somehow, he'd figure out how to reel her back in—get that feeling back again, the one he only ever had with her.

He had no intention of committing. To anyone. But he convinced himself that the casual fling he'd had with Monique was top tier, and he could simply slip right back into that role again. Maybe even convince her to sing at the Cyder Lounge again, exactly like it had been before.

Then he remembered Sarah. Sweet little Sarah, who he'd been tagging along with for months now. Keeping her at arm's length. Always turning up unannounced at her house for sex, but never taking her on a date—because then it would start to feel real.

He was trapped in a relationship he was only pretending to be in. And he knew that bubble would have to burst at some point. But not yet.

"When are we going to meet Sarah, mate?" Chris asked a few nights later.

Chris, Tony, and two other tagalongs were having pre-drinks at David's house before getting ready to hit the town. David had no intention of going near the Cyder Lounge tonight. In fact, he'd been spending less and less time there lately. Knowing his dad transferred him the equivalent of a full-time wage every month—no matter how much or little he worked—did little to motivate him, despite his dad's repeated calls.

"Never," David snapped. "I'd never feed her to a pack of hungry wolves like you lot."

"Oh come on, mate. I thought you might share her around. I mean, things aren't actually serious with you two, right?"

David's blood boiled. This wasn't the first time these guys joked like that about his one-night flings, but this was different. He felt an overwhelming need to protect Sarah from the world's harsh edges. Little did she know, she was already encased within the confines of his own steely shell.

"I've changed my mind. I'm not heading out tonight."

"David. Seriously? You're going to leave us hanging again, bro? What's up with you these days?"

"I'm just not feeling it."

"We depend on you, mate. A night out on the piss is way too expensive these days."

Monique's words filtered through his mind. He hesitated before asking, "So, you're just using me for free drinks. Is that it?"

Silence. Dead silence. No one in the room could even look him in the eye.

"Do any of you even like me? Chris? Tony?"

"Sure we do," Tony said, with zero conviction.

"Out! Get out! All of you!"

He felt like the world was crumbling around him. He didn't need those hangers-on taking advantage of him. But he couldn't sit here alone, dwelling on his own thoughts. His first instinct was to go to Monique's house. But he didn't want to be another Shane, hassling her at home. She deserved better than that. So, Sarah's house was the next best choice.

After the blow-up with the boys and Monique's voice still echoing in his head, he needed something familiar. Something soft. Sarah was that—sweet, predictable Sarah. She never pushed back. Never made him feel like he was too much.

He knocked once. Then again. Finally, the door opened.

Sarah looked stunning in black pants and a red one-shoulder top. She looked good. Really good. But she didn't smile when she saw him. That was new.

"Well, look who's all dressed up with nowhere to go," he said, slipping an arm around her waist like he always did.

She pulled away. That stung.

"Oh David, what are you doing here?"

"Just thought I'd be a considerate boyfriend and pop by for a visit!" He leaned in for a kiss, but she turned her cheek. Another sting.

"Aww, that's sweet, but Lauren and I were actually about to head out."

His stomach tightened. "Go out? Go out where?"

She hesitated. He could see it. "We're meeting up with some friends for drinks."

Friends. That could mean anything. "Would there be male friends there by any chance?"

She threw up her hands. "Well, yes!"

And just like that, the switch flipped. He couldn't help it. The thought of other guys looking at her, touching her, laughing with her—it made his blood boil. And the conversation he'd just had with Chris and Tony—the way they talked about her—enflamed him.

"Then I don't want you to go. I don't trust other guys putting their dirty hands all over you."

"David!" she snapped, eyes flashing. "You can't tell me what to do. I'm just meeting up with friends. What's wrong with that? You do it all the time!"

She was right. But that didn't matter. Logic didn't matter. The idea of her out there, vulnerable, made him feel like he was losing control.

"I don't trust them. You're like my perfect little flower, Sarah. I don't want anyone trying to take you away from me."

He meant it as a compliment, but the way she recoiled told him he'd missed the mark. Again.

"No one's going to take me from you, David. I love you, but you have to stop being so controlling."

That word—controlling—hit harder than he expected. He wasn't trying to control her. He was trying to protect her. Wasn't he? And every time she said I love you, he could feel himself sinking deeper into the pit of his own grave.

"I don't care; I don't like this one bit. Come on, baby, just stay here with me tonight. We can have the whole night alone together!"

He reached for her again, desperate now. Music from Lauren's room blasted through the walls—some pop song he didn't recognise. It made everything feel louder. Messier.

Sarah stood firm. "I'm going out with my friends tonight, David. You either trust me or you don't. The choice is yours. Either way, I've made plans and I'm going to keep them this time."

He blinked. She'd never spoken to him like that before. Not once. She was always the one who bent, who made room for him. But not tonight.

Over his shoulder, he caught Lauren peeking through her bedroom door, clearly enjoying the show. That made it worse.

"You ready, Lauren?" Sarah called out, her voice steady, her eyes locked on his.

"Oh, I'm so ready!" Lauren chirped, sweeping into the room like she was walking a red carpet.

David didn't move. Couldn't. His body felt heavy, like he'd been hit with something invisible. Sarah brushed past him, calm and composed, and he just stood there, watching her go.

"I love you, baby. But I have to live my life too."

She said it like it was final. Like she was choosing herself over him. And maybe she was.

He watched them walk out into the night, arm in arm, laughing like he hadn't just been gutted. He wanted to call after her, to say something clever or cruel or desperate. But nothing came.

Instead, he turned slowly, head bowed, and walked back to his car. The engine was cold. So was he.

She'd stood up to him. And he didn't know whether to admire her or resent her for it.

All he knew was that something had shifted. And he wasn't sure he could shift with it.

David slid into the driver's seat, gripping the wheel like it might anchor him. He twisted the keys into the ignition and turned the radio on. **"If You Could Read My Mind" by Ultra Naté, Amber, and Jocelyn Enriquez** played, causing David's thoughts to spiral—Sarah laughing with her friends, Sarah dancing with someone else, Sarah slipping further and further away from him.

He hated that feeling. That slow, gnawing panic that came when something he wanted started slipping through his fingers.

He could go after her. Show up at the bar. Pretend it was a coincidence. But that would make him look desperate. Worse—unhinged.

And he wasn't that guy. Was he?

He leaned his head back against the seat, eyes closed. The twisted metaphor he'd thrown at her—"perfect little flower"—made him cringe. What the hell was that? He sounded like a villain in a bad romance novel. No wonder she looked at him like he'd grown horns.

He didn't want to be that guy. The one who showed up uninvited, who made her feel small, who tried to control what she wore and where she went. But he also didn't know how to be anything else. Not when the fear of losing her felt bigger than anything else.

David started the engine, the low hum filling the silence. He didn't drive off right away. Just sat there, staring at the empty footpath where Sarah had stood minutes ago.

She was right. He had to trust her.

But trust wasn't something he gave easily. Not after Monique. Not after watching his mum walk out without a goodbye. Not after years of pretending he didn't care when he cared too damn much.

He pulled away from the curb slowly, headlights slicing through the night.

He didn't know where he was going. Maybe nowhere. Maybe just away from the version of himself he didn't want to be anymore.

Chapter 19

Monique

Monique sat on the edge of her bed, folding a stack of freshly laundered clothes that still smelled faintly of Surf powder and eucalyptus while listening and singing along to **"Break Me Shake Me" by Savage Garden**. The fan above her clicked with every rotation, a lazy rhythm that matched the heat outside.

She paused, one leg of denim dangling from her hand, and stared at her Nokia 3210 buzzing on the doona beside her. One new message.

David: *Sry abt what I said.*

Her stomach tightened. He had some nerve texting her after that phone call — after throwing out that cruel line about her having no friends.

She had friends. Now. Julie was her friend.

Still, those words echoed louder than they should. She'd replayed them more times than she cared to admit.

Another buzz.

David: *U do have friends.*

David: *Me. If u want.*

She rolled her eyes. Classic David. Apologising like it was a dare.

And every message cost her twenty-five cents—logged on her paper bill with time and number like a trail of emotional receipts. She only had room to save ten, so she'd been ruthless about which ones stayed. Why was she even considering keeping this one? She picked up the phone, thumb hovering over the buttons.

Monique: *lol. Thats rich.*

David: *I'm serious.*

Monique: *No ur not.*

David: *Yes I am. BF 4eva <3*

Monique winced. That line should've come with a hazard warning.

Monique: *Bye David.*

Monique stared at the screen, thumb hovering over the keypad.

She rolled her eyes so hard it was practically aerobic. Then, without thinking, she tossed the Nokia across the room. It hit the wall with a satisfying thunk, bounced off the skirting board, and landed face down on the carpet.

She didn't flinch. Didn't even blink.

Just reached over, picked it up, and flipped it over like nothing had happened. Screen still glowing. Message still intact.

She wished her resolve was as indestructible as that damn phone — because why, *why*, was there a flush of warmth in her cheeks?

The next day, Monique sat cross-legged on the front steps of her townhouse, a half-melted Rainbow Paddle Pop dripping down her wrist. The cicadas were loud today, buzzing like faulty speakers in the trees. Across the street, two kids zipped past on Razor scooters, their wheels clacking over the uneven footpath.

Inside, *Video Hits* was playing on the TV — **"Heartbreaker" by Mariah Carey** again. That song was haunting her today. It had followed her from the servo to the corner shop, like some kind of cosmic joke.

Her Nokia buzzed in her lap. She admired her translucent pink phone case and glittering gold buttons before bringing the tiny screen to her face for a closer look.

David: *Wats 4 lnch?*

She stared at the screen in one hand, glanced at the melting Paddle Pop in the other, and cringed. Typical David. Out of the blue. No context. Just barging into her day like he was always meant to be part of it.

She considered ignoring it. But she was alone — again — and in the mood for a bit of light banter.

She threw the rest of her ice cream in the nearby wheelie bin and typed back.

Monique: *Not a burrito, if that's what ur fishing 4.*

David: *Was hoping 4 a chip. Or 2.*

Monique: *Buy ur own.*

David: *Mine taste better when stolen.*

Monique: *U always did have a talent 4 theft.*

David: *Only hearts.*

Monique: *-_-*

David: *Still got mine. U want it back?*

Monique: *Nope*

David: *Bit dented. Still beats 4 u tho ;)*

What kind of game was this? Absolutely deplorable. These lines shouldn't be working on her—and yet, somehow, her heart fluttered at the sight of a few letters scattered across the screen. She could practically see David's cocky grin as he stared down at his phone, typing that message like he knew exactly what it would do to her.

Monique: *U been watching Titanic again?*

David: *Maybe. Leo's hair inspired me.*

Monique: *U wish.*

David: *Can I CU?*

Monique: *No.*

David: *K. I'll wait.*

She pegged the phone across her lawn, knowing perfectly well that it would still be sitting in the grass, undamaged as always. She walked over and picked it up, brushing off the grass and dirt. She really should treat her mobile phone better, but David had a way of forcing her to inflict involuntary abuse on her poor Nokia.

The sun was dipping low, casting long shadows across the pavement. A couple walked past holding hands, laughing about something she couldn't hear.

Buzz.

David: *Cyder Lounge misses u*

Monique: *Can't. Not human*

David: *CU there 2nite? Say hi to Sam*

Monique: *Nice try.*

David: *You miss it. Come. 4 old times sake ;)*

Monique: *If I say no?*

David: *I'll B there. Waiting. Up 2 U. Would be gr8 2 CU x*

Oof. He pressed her buttons. Why did he have to bring up the Cyder Lounge?

She'd been circling the question for a while now, wondering if she'd been too brash, too proud, too quick to walk away from something that still tugged at her. Singing. Because she craved it. Missed it. The pulse of it. The way it made her feel seen.

If she met him there—and it was a big if—It was just reconnaissance — a quiet way to gauge whether the door she'd slammed shut might still open. But beneath the logic, she knew the truth.

A postie drove up to her letterbox in his motorbike to deliver the mail. She walked over, pulled out the wad of letters and sifted through them until one made her pause and look closer.

Dear Ms Chambers,

We write in relation to the estate of your late mother, Mrs Catherine Chambers, who passed away on 14 January 1998.

Our records indicate an outstanding tax liability of $1,842.65 relating to the 1996–1997 financial year. This amount includes accrued interest and late lodgement penalties.

As executor of the estate, you are responsible for ensuring that this debt is settled in full prior to the distribution of assets...

At the sight of her mother's name, she was transported right back there. Catherine's frail body lying helpless in that hospital bed. Staying by her side until her final breath. The loneliness that settled in and never quite left.

She didn't care about the money. She'd pull from her dismal travel savings, again, and put that dream off even further. But the helplessness, the fear, the sorrow bundled into that letter had her reeling.

She didn't want to be alone. Couldn't be alone with these thoughts.

She needed a distraction, and would it be such a bad thing if David were the only one offering the company she needed in this moment?

She knew it could be dangerous. She knew where interactions like this had led her before. But she was willing to risk it, just to quiet the ache and replace it with something else.

She opened the phone again. Typed slowly.

Monique: *CU @ Cyder 2nite :-)*

And hit send.

Was she ready to go back? Too late. She'd set the scene for history to repeat. She hoped she wouldn't regret it.

Chapter 20

Monique

The familiar warmth of the Cyder Lounge wrapped around Monique like a friendly hug. It hadn't changed a bit.

As she stepped inside, heels clicking against polished hardwood, the stage where she'd performed caught her eye—that same stage where she'd finally begun living her dream, where her voice had filled this upscale space and caught more than just the audience's attention. She remembered how David had watched her that first night, his eyes following her every move as she'd sung her heart out.

She used to sing here. Used to feel like she belonged.

Then David happened.

And everything got messy.

Monday nights were quiet, but loyal. The kind of crowd that didn't need a show, just a drink and a familiar corner.

The leopard print dress hugged her curves like armour.

She didn't dress for him.

But she couldn't deny knowing the effect this dress would have on him.

What was she doing here? After all these months, after he'd made it crystal clear that keeping his options open was the priority. Yet here she sat, in this leopard print dress that made her feel simultaneously powerful and exposed, waiting for a man who she already walked away from to protect herself.

Samuel Sparks was behind the bar, clipboard in hand, muttering like always. When he saw her, his face softened.

"Monique," he called gently.

She offered a polite smile. "Hi, Sam."

"You should sing again sometime. Crowd misses you."

She shrugged. "We'll see."

She missed the stage with a quiet ache. But wanting it and being ready for it and the mess that came along with it were two very different things.

Then she saw him.

David.

Leaning against the bar like he owned the place. Technically, he didn't. But he wore it like he did.

Monique noticed **"Everywhere You Go" by Taxiride** playing on the speakers as David's eyes locked onto hers, and the air shifted.

She hated that.

Hated how her body still responded before her brain could catch up.

"You came," he said, voice low.

"I said I would."

"You look..." He paused, drinking her in. "...amazing."

She raised a brow. "And you look like a man who still thinks he can get whatever he wants with a few text messages."

"I wasn't playing games," he said. "I just didn't know how else to reach you."

"So you try being... what, sweet?" Her smile tightened. "Since when do you ask girls how their day was?"

"I missed you."

That caught her off guard.

She blinked. "Really."

"I've been trying to forget you," he said. "I've had options."

Of course he had.

She laughed, but it came out hollow. "Girls fall over themselves for that smirk and a pretty line."

"But it's not the same." He stepped closer. "It's not you."

She studied him, heart thudding. Her brain screamed at her to maintain distance, to remember the nights she'd spent trying to convince herself she was better off without him. But her body remembered other nights, ones filled with passion and promises that had felt real in the darkness.

"You don't get to say that," she said quietly. "Not after the way you kept me at arm's length. Made me feel like I was the only one catching real feelings."

"I was scared," he admitted. "Of how much I wanted you. Of what that meant."

"And what does it mean now?"

"That I still want you. That I can't stop wanting you."

His gaze was steady. "That I don't care how long it takes—I'll wait."

Her walls cracked. Just slightly. The words she was afraid to hear months ago now felt like both a balm and a threat to the walls she'd carefully constructed.

"You still don't know what you want, David."

"I do now."

She looked away, exhaling slowly.

"Everything about you is dangerous," she whispered. "You walk into a room, and I forget why I ever told myself to stay away."

He stepped closer. Inches away.

"Then don't stay away."

Her hands trembled at her sides.

But her body leaned in before her mind could protest.

"I shouldn't do this," she said.

"You want to."

"That's not the same as trusting you."

"I know," he said softly. "But maybe... this is a start."

He didn't push. Just waited. She closed the distance. The kiss was inevitable. Slow. Intentional.

It tasted like memory and regret and everything unfinished.

She hated how good it felt.

Hated how easily she melted into him.

When they finally pulled apart, her breath caught.

"This doesn't mean I'm back," she said.

"I'm not asking for that," he replied. "I'm just asking you not to leave. Not tonight."

She looked at him, lips parted, heart racing.

"Then don't screw it up," she murmured.

The irony wasn't lost on her—how this place that had represented her dreams of a singing career had also led her to David, a man who'd become both her sweetest melody and her most conflicting note. But for now, she chose to silence her doubts. To believe, just for this moment, that sometimes people really do change. That sometimes, what breaks your heart can also be what heals it.

Chapter 21

David

David drifted in the hazy space between sleep and consciousness, aware of Monique's warmth beside him—a feeling he'd dreamed about countless times since she walked away last year. Even half-asleep, his body recognised her presence, craved it. This was right. This was what he'd wanted all along, even when he'd been too stubborn, too afraid to admit it.

The violent impact of something hitting his chest jolted him awake.

His phone.

Monique stood at the foot of his bed, gloriously naked and absolutely furious. The sight would have been arousing if not for the look of pure betrayal in her eyes.

"Sarah?!" Her voice cut through his grogginess like a knife. "Who's Sarah, huh?"

The name hit him like a bucket of ice water.

Sarah.

Christ.

In the intoxicating whirlwind of finally having Monique back in his arms, he'd completely forgotten about Sarah. Shame and panic collided in his chest as he watched Monique gathering her clothes, her movements sharp with anger.

"What are you talking about, baby? Come back to bed." The words tumbled out automatically, a desperate attempt to delay the inevitable explosion. But even as he said them, he knew it was useless. Monique had always been too smart to fall for his charm when she was truly angry.

"Your girlfriend is calling you." The accusation hung in the air like poison.

Reality crashed down around him as he scrambled out of bed. Sarah wasn't his girlfriend—not really. She was a distraction, a poor attempt to fill the Monique-shaped hole in his life. He'd fallen into it without meaning to, letting Sarah believe there was more between them than there really was, because it was easier than facing how badly he'd screwed things up with the woman he really wanted.

"Wait, baby," he pleaded, reaching for Monique with a desperation that surprised even him. "You've got it all wrong. She's nobody. You're my girl. There's nobody else but you."

The words were true—painfully, absurdly true. This was the moment his heart decided to voice it? Monique had always been the one, even when he'd been too afraid to commit, too caught up in his own ego to admit it.

Her cold stare cut through his excuses.

"You better not be two-timing me, David. You have no idea what I'm capable of."

He tried to approach her, instinctively falling back on the seduction that had always worked before.

"You've got it all wrong, babe. Just hear me out..."

But she shoved him away, and the force of it felt like judgment for every mistake he'd made.

She was right to be angry. He'd done this—created this mess because he couldn't commit to her months ago, couldn't admit that she was everything he wanted. And now, just when he'd finally gotten her back, his past decisions were destroying everything again.

"Don't try to sweet-talk your way out of this," she spat, and he saw the hurt beneath her anger. The pain he'd caused—yet again.

He opened his mouth, desperate to explain. To tell her that Sarah meant nothing. That these past months without Monique had been torture. That he'd finally understood what an idiot he'd been.

The knock at the door silenced everything.

David's heart stopped as he watched the scene unfold like a slow-motion car crash. Monique opened the door to find Sarah—sweet, innocent Sarah—standing there in her sunny dress, looking like everything Monique wasn't. And Monique—fierce, passionate Monique—regarded her with a mixture of pity and disgust that made him want to crawl out of his own skin.

"Sarah, I presume?" Monique's whisper carried more judgment than a scream.

He stood paralysed, half-naked in the hallway, as Monique brushed past Sarah and walked away. The sound of her car starting up outside finally broke his trance.

The weight of his choices pressed down on him like a physical thing as he noticed the radio in his living room play **"If You Had My Love" by Jennifer Lopez**.

He'd finally gotten what he wanted—Monique back in his arms, in his bed, in his life. And in less than twelve hours, he'd destroyed it all over again.

Only this time, he knew with crushing certainty: there would be no coming back from this.

He'd seen it in her eyes—this wasn't just anger or hurt. This was the end.

David walked to the door and watched Monique's car screech away, leaving him frozen with Sarah's devastated face before him. The sound of her retreating footsteps snapped him into action. He couldn't chase after Monique—she was already gone, probably for good this time.

But Sarah... Sarah was here. And the look of betrayal on her face was like a knife to his gut.

"Sarah, wait!" The words burst from him as she turned and fled down the stairs. Without thinking about his state of undress—wearing nothing but black satin boxers—he bounded after her. The concrete was rough against his bare feet, but the physical discomfort was nothing compared to the crushing weight of guilt in his chest.

"Please, let me explain!" The words sounded hollow even to his own ears. What could he possibly say? That he'd never meant to hurt her? That she'd been a bandage for his wounded heart after Monique left? That even though his feelings for her weren't as deep as hers for him, he'd genuinely cared?

The morning sun beat down on his bare shoulders as he pursued her, aware of how ridiculous he must look—a grown man in his underwear chasing a girl in a yellow polka dot dress down the street. But he couldn't let her leave like this. He owed her... something. An explanation. An apology. Anything.

The sudden screech of wheels against pavement made him wince as Sarah dragged a wheelie bin into his path. Before he could process what was happening, she toppled it over, sending its putrid contents spilling across the sidewalk. The stench of rotting garbage hit him like a wall.

"Screw you, David! You cheating cheater!" Her voice cracked with hurt and fury as she flipped him off—the gesture so at odds with her sweet dress and the sunflower on her denim jacket that it would've been comical if it weren't so heartbreaking.

He tried to navigate around the mess, his bare feet carefully avoiding the scattered garbage, but the delay cost him precious seconds. Sarah was pulling ahead, her blonde hair streaming behind her like a banner of accusation. His chest heaved with exertion and emotion as he pushed himself to catch up.

But with each step, the futility of his chase became clearer.

What would he even say if he caught her? How could he explain that his heart had always belonged to someone else, even when he was with her? That he'd tried to move on, tried to be the man she deserved, but had failed spectacularly?

His legs gave out beneath him, and he collapsed onto his hands and knees on the rough concrete. The physical pain barely registered through the emotional turmoil. He watched Sarah's figure grow smaller in the distance, her yellow dress a diminishing spot of brightness against the grey morning.

David remained there on his knees, the concrete burning against his skin, garbage strewn behind him and two broken hearts ahead of him. In trying to have everything, he'd ended up with nothing. Monique was gone—this time forever, he was certain. And Sarah... sweet, undeserving Sarah, who'd only ever given him kindness, was fleeing from him like he was a monster.

Maybe he was.

The morning traffic began to pick up, curious onlookers slowing to gawk at the half-naked man kneeling on the sidewalk. David barely noticed them. All he could see was the damage he'd caused—Monique's cold fury, Sarah's shattered innocence. He'd managed to destroy both relationships in the span of ten minutes, and the worst part was, he had no one to blame but himself.

The sun continued to rise over the suburb, indifferent to the drama that had just unfolded beneath it.

David finally pushed himself to his feet, his knees scraped and his dignity in tatters. The walk back to his house felt longer than the chase had been, each step a reminder of his failures. Behind him, the scattered garbage marked the path of his latest mistake like breadcrumbs of shame.

Chapter 22

Monique

Monique was supposed to go to work today. But how was she meant to show up in this unhinged emotional state?

What a fool she'd been. She cranked **"Linger" by The Cranberries** to full volume on her car's CD player, the haunting vocals slicing through the morning air like truth. To think David might've changed. To think this could've turned into something real — and he had a girlfriend.

An *actual* girlfriend. She was rattled. Spun out of her mind.

Mr Untethered had somehow managed to get himself tied down. Not very securely, though, if he was still chasing Monique on the side.

What an absolute pig.

She felt disgusted. Humiliated. Sick to her stomach. But no—she didn't cry.

She was angry.

Revenge flashed through her mind like a neon sign. She glanced down at David's wallet sitting on the passenger seat and smiled. Wicked. Unapologetic. She snatched it up from the desk by the door while he wasn't looking. It was too easy.

As she drove her maroon Honda Legend across the Story Bridge, Monique admired the skyscrapers rising beside her and the massive river stretching below. She rolled the window all the way down. The wind whipped at her hair.

She grabbed the wallet, leaned out, and hurled it toward the river below with everything she had.

Woosh. Gone.

And just like that, she felt better. Not healed. But better.

Still, that was just the beginning. For her — and for that poor girl who'd stood in the open doorway, staring back at Monique with wide, betrayed eyes — she had more in store. Tactics. Plans. Ways to make him hurt.

Things were about to get messy.

David wouldn't live this down. Not ever.

David

Ring-ring.

Kyle dropped his shopping bags at the front door and reached for the phone nearby.

"No! Don't answer that!" David yelled in desperation from the other side of the room.

Kyle hadn't been home for nearly a week—been staying at some chick's house, apparently—so he had no idea of the torture he was about to endure.

He gave David a *What's wrong with you?* look. Because who doesn't automatically answer the phone when it rings? What if it was important? Answering the house phone was usually a given—but not in this hellish scenario.

"Hello? ...Oh no, I don't have time to do your survey. Sorry. Can you take this number off your list, please? Thanks."

"That's not going to work, you know."

"What are you talking about? These companies legally have to take our number off their list now. I should know." Of course, Mr Lawyer Man would use this opportunity to remind David of his law degree.

"I already tried that, but it didn't work. This is the tenth time they've called today. By the way, I also need a new credit card, driver's licence, and Medicare card. How do I sort that out?"

"How you function as an adult is beyond me. What did you do, David?"

"I don't want to talk about it. So, are you gonna help me or not?"

"No, David. Man up and figure it out yourself." Kyle picked up the grocery bags and walked to the kitchen. "Or give your dad a call. Ask him. You've been avoiding the Cyder Lounge and Sammy like the plague lately, and he's been desperate to get a hold of you. Why haven't you been answering his calls?"

"I've just been... busy."

It was true. He'd been distant. Vacant. Pushing himself away from the world he knew, piece by piece, until there was no world left. Just oblivion. He was in a dark place, and this scandal of his own creation with Monique and Sarah had sunk him deeper into the hole.

But he had to keep it in. Save face. Make it look like he was in control. And maybe—just maybe—the confident man others saw on the outside would somehow seep through his bones and fix the mess unravelling inside.

David stared down at his Nokia, barely registering Kyle's voice from the kitchen. Kyle mentioned inviting someone over later—someone he wanted David to meet.

David muttered, "Oh yeah," just to be polite, despite giving zero fucks.

His head was swimming with too many thoughts.

He'd been sending texts and voice messages to both Sarah and Monique for days now. Saying sorry. Probably coming across like a real overbearing jackass. But he didn't know what else to do to fix this. Balancing two girls at once was always going to end badly.

And then—a message from Sarah flashed on his screen.

Sarah: *Meet me uni 2day @ 12.*

He had to go. See her face-to-face. Explain himself.

Chapter 23

David

David's palms were slick as he paced the paved entrance to the university campus. Yeah, he was nervous. This wasn't like brushing off a one-night stand—this cut deeper. The stakes were real.

A car idled nearby, windows down, blasting **"Gotta Tell You" by Samantha Mumba.** The beat thumped against his chest like a second heartbeat.

Then he saw her.

Sarah.

Her face unreadable, her stride fast and deliberate. No hesitation. No softness. Just a woman on a mission—and he was the destination.

And then she was there—standing right in front of him.

David reached out, instinctively, fingertips brushing the air between them. His go-to move. A gentle touch to her cheek, the soft look that always calmed her when she started to unravel. It had worked before. Every time. She'd melt, fold into his arms like forgiveness was inevitable.

But not this time.

She swatted his hand away, sharp and final.

Something had shifted.

The look in her eyes wasn't the wounded vulnerability he'd grown used to managing. No trace of the hurt puppy he'd comforted and controlled. This was something he'd only ever seen a glimpse of before.

This was resolve.

"I can't believe I ever thought I loved you," she said, each word deliberate, each syllable landing like a slap. "I'm only here so that I can tell you to your face that it's over between us, and you need to stop calling me."

David felt his carefully constructed mask slip. This wasn't how things were supposed to go. Sarah was predictable, controllable—that's why he kept her around despite never really wanting a girlfriend. After ruining what he could have with Monique, keeping Sarah within his own tightly controlled circle had given him back some sense of power.

"Oh, baby, you don't mean that," he tried, forcing confidence into his voice that he didn't feel.

Her response was immediate, cutting. "Oh, believe me, I do!"

The triumphant smile on her face caught him off guard. This wasn't his Sarah—the insecure girl who would forgive anything just to keep him. This was someone new, someone he couldn't manipulate.

He tried to maintain his composure, but panic was rising in his chest. He needed her to stay. Not because he loved her—he never had—but because without her, he'd have to face the emptiness again.

That void that had opened up when his mother left, the one he'd been filling with booze and women ever since. The same emptiness that had terrified him when Monique had gotten too close, making him sabotage everything with her in fear of falling too deep for something real. Something that he secretly wanted to last, but he knew it never could. Because nothing ever did. And here with Sarah in this moment only proved that fact.

He could see the change in Sarah as she stood there. Her head held high, eyes sparkling with something he'd never seen in them before—freedom. The realisation that he was losing his grip on her made him desperate.

"Sarah, come on. We can work this out." He was throwing out anything he could think of, watching it all bounce off her newfound armour.

She just smiled, a real smile that didn't need his approval to exist. "I'm seeing someone else now, David, so you can drop it. I've moved on, and it's time for you to do the same."

The words hit him like a physical blow. Someone else? Michael, that bloke from her university class, perhaps? The thought of being replaced so easily by some tertiary-educated wanker bruised his ego far more than it should have. She was supposed to be waiting for him, always available when Monique wouldn't have him.

As she turned to leave, he called after her, pride abandoned. "Sarah, wait! You can't just—"

But she was already walking away, his pleas echoing uselessly behind her. The finality of her exit left him standing alone, the familiar emptiness rushing back in.

He wanted to be angry, to blame her. But somewhere beneath the wounded ego and practised charm, he knew the truth. This was his fault. He'd used her to feel something, anything, after Monique had shown him what it really meant to feel something. He'd been so terrified of that intensity that he'd ruined everything, hurting anyone who got close.

Just like he had always done since his mother left.

David pulled out his Nokia, scrolling to Monique's number. Maybe if he called her, explained things... But what would he say? Would he say that seeing Sarah walk away made him realise how much worse it had felt when Monique did the same? That he'd been trying to fill a void his mother left with meaningless conquests and alcohol?

He put the phone away and walked to the nearest bar—deliberately steering clear of the Cyder Lounge. Another drink would be easier. It always was.

Chapter 24

David

David fumbled through the doorway, swung his arm toward the key hook and missed. The keys hit the floor with a metallic clatter.

"Hello!"

David looked up, eyes unsteady to see an unfamiliar woman sitting on the couch. Petite and smiling with a butterfly on her shirt and two messy dark-brown buns secured to the top of her head.

"Hello?" David replied, suddenly unsure if he'd stumbled into the wrong house in his inebriated state.

Then Kyle appeared from the kitchen, casually carrying a cheeseboard.

"Oh good, you're back. This is Cara." Kyle stood behind the couch and laid a hand on her shoulder.

"Nice to meet you...*burrp!*" David stumbled to the couch across from her and flopped into it like a dead weight.

Kyle put the cheeseboard onto the coffee table and stood over David with a disapproving glare.

"Drunk? Really? It's 3 o'clock in the afternoon on a Wednesday." His voice was hushed, as if trying to hide the obvious from the chick sitting opposite him.

"Yeah. So..."

"I was hoping you'd be sober. I wanted you to meet my new girlfriend."

David scoffed, "Girlfriend? You? Really? Fuck Off."

"Yeah. Well. We met at a costume party. I was Jack from Titanic. She was Rose. Meant to be. Have been going out for about three months now." David looked up at Kyle and across at Cara. Their expressions unreadable. Oh, he wasn't kidding.

"Well, woopdie fucking do." David did not have the brain capacity or sobriety to handle this right now. He knew he was being rude, but he was fuelled entirely by emotions and impulse. Logic and forethought had withered away entirely three schooners ago.

Water. He needed water.

David arched forward, reaching for the coffee table to steady himself as he stood — but instead of hitting wood, his palm slammed into the edge of the platter.

Cheese, cold meats, crackers, and olives went flying, scattering across the table and onto the floor

"Oh Shit. Sorry."

Kyle let out a long, exasperated sigh. "Cara darling. I think we'll have to do this another time."

"It's okay, want me to help tidy this up?"

"No, I think it's best if you head back home and I'll come by shortly. I just need to have a quick chat with David."

David crouched, picking food up off the floor to put back on the table, filled with too much self-loathing to acknowledge the conversation going on around him.

Once Cara left, Kyle crouched until he was level with David's eyes. "I can't keep watching you do this to yourself."

"What are you talking about? You don't really care about me." David shifted away, scooped the last two pieces of cheese off the floor and shoved them into his mouth.

Kyle stood, looming. "I don't care about you? I'm your best friend."

David rose to look down at him. "Pffft. Dream on, loser." He walked to the kitchen, grabbed the glass of water he'd been craving and gulped it down as if trying to wash the words away. Best friend? Who did Kyle think he was?

"I'm moving out."

David dropped his cup in the sink with a loud clatter. "What?"

"You heard me. I'm going to move in with Cara."

"After three months? Really?"

"Yes. And it's got to be better than living with your sorry ass!" Kyle snapped.

"I know you've been through a lot, and I've tried to be here for you but...you keep pushing me away."

"Because you're a *loser* Kyle. Who would want to be friends with *you*?"

"Am I? Speak for yourself. I'm making something of myself. I'm going to be a lawyer and you're just here floundering, fucking around and drinking all the time and I just can't watch you destroy yourself like this anymore."

"I don't need you telling me how to live my life."

"It seems like someone has to. Your dad's worried about you too. Has been for a long time. That's why he asked me to live with you." He what? David had the sudden urge to fill up that cup of water again and throw it in Kyle's smug face.

"*He* asked *you* to live with *me*? Like I'm some kind of charity case that needs constant supervision? That's not a friend. That's a fucking mole."

"Okay, whatever. Good riddance. I'm out. I'll be back over the next few days to get the rest of my stuff."

"Good. Get out. I don't want you here."

Once Kyle had grabbed a few things and slammed the door behind him, David was left standing in the kitchen. Alone. Thoroughly and completely alone.

His thoughts spiralled into self-loathing as he drifted back into the lounge room. He flicked on the radio and collapsed onto the couch, staring at the destroyed cheeseboard Kyle had clearly prepared to share with him and his new girlfriend — probably in anticipation of introducing her to David. His best friend.

Then the music hit him.

He scoffed as he recognised the track: **"Better Off Alone" by Alice Deejay.**

Of course. Even the radio was mocking him now.

David stared at the spread. Cheese, crackers, cold meats. He picked up a slice of brie and took a bite. It tasted sour on his tongue.

He treated everyone around him like shit. Sarah. Kyle. Monique. Sammy. The hate and anger he carried spilled out of him, infecting everything he touched. He couldn't contain it. Couldn't stop it.

He was a broken man. Had been for years. Ever since his mother left, his self-worth had been shattered beyond repair. He'd been trying to patch it together with ego and bravado, hoping it would drown out the truth — that he was worthless. That no one really wanted him.

He kept eating. Bite after bite, as if the food might fill the hollow space inside him. He didn't stop until he was nearly bursting at the seams.

Maybe this was who he really was. Maybe that song was right. He was better off alone.

Early the next morning, the sun barely risen, David was startled awake from his restless sleep. The shrill ring of the house phone shattered the silence. He let it ring out as he tossed and turned. Eventually, his father's voice crackled through the answering machine, urgent and clipped, pulling David from the edge of unconsciousness.

"David. I need you at the Cyder Lounge right now. This is bad. Really bad."

What the fuck?

David rubbed his eyes, stumbling out into the lounge room.

He expected to see Kyle's head pop out from his bedroom, looking far perkier than he felt, until he remembered Kyle had gone and he was alone. The memory was somehow making his hangover feel even worse. He had no idea what he was about to walk into.

The street was quiet at 5 am, save for the low hum of a garbage truck groaning its way down the block. As the cab turned the corner onto the nightclub strip, he was faced with police cars, yellow tape and devastation beyond words.

The Cyder Lounge looked gutted.

The front windows were smashed in, jagged shards glittering like ice. Spray-painted across the sandstone façade in thick, angry strokes were two words: MAN WHORE

Inside, the bar was a war zone. Velvet booths slashed open, stuffing spilling like entrails. Liquor bottles shattered across the floor. The grand piano was overturned, keys broken like teeth.

David froze. His first thought—*Monique?* He'd broken her heart, and she responded with incessant telemarketer calls and a stolen wallet.

But this? This was utter annihilation.

He couldn't imagine she'd have the capacity for something like this.

Samuel Sparks emerged. His tailored shirt was rumpled, sleeves rolled up, face pale and drawn. He looked at David like he was seeing a ghost.

"You did this," Samuel said, voice low and trembling.

David blinked. "I just got here."

"No," Samuel snapped. "Not with your hands. But with your bloody charm. Your flings. Your goddamn ego."

David opened his mouth, but Samuel raised a hand.

"I warned you, didn't I? You think you can fuck around, bedding patrons like it's a sport? Some of these women have husbands. Boyfriends. Business partners. You think they wouldn't retaliate?"

David's jaw tightened as he remained tight lipped.

"I don't care who did it," Samuel continued. "I care that it's your fault. And I'm done paying for your mess."

David flinched. "What are you saying?"

"I'm cutting you off. No more weekly transfers. No more free rides. You want money? Earn it. Do a full day's work. Hell, do *any* work."

Silence hung between them, thick as smoke.

David looked around, heart thudding. The damage wasn't just physical—it was personal. Every broken bottle, every slur on the wall, was a mirror held up to his worst self.

And somewhere, maybe Monique was laughing. Or crying. Or both.

Chapter 25

Monique

Monique had finally gotten her focus back at work. But that focus had narrowed into one very specific task: making sure David's home phone number stayed in the call team's rotation.

It was a brilliant revenge idea — though credit went to Julie. Monique only wished she'd thought of it herself.

Sure, there was a risk of getting caught, but Janice never checked that kind of thing. And Monique planned to pull the number as soon as she felt his torture had reached a satisfying level. Janice would be none the wiser.

Every time a caller deleted his number from the system—per his request—Monique simply added it back in manually.

That would show him.

The only thing worse than working in a call centre? Being on the receiving end of one that refuses to leave you alone.

She'd been smug about it for days. Every time David's number popped back into the system, she felt a flicker of satisfaction.

Julie called it petty brilliance. Monique called it closure.

But closure had a price.

"You're fired."

"What?"

"You heard me. You're fired."

Janice looked like she'd swallowed a firecracker, cheeks flushed and hands on her hips. "You deliberately broke the code of conduct to get back at some ex. Really? I thought you were better than that."

She did too.

The way David got into her head — under her skin — was obscene. She'd gone so far as to sacrifice her own financial security just to get revenge. How pathetic.

But how did Janice know? She never monitored that kind of thing.

David must have reported it.

Monique's heart sank. She knew what she did wasn't right, but she never imagined David would be the type to dob her in.

Then again, she'd been wrong about him before. And clearly, she was wrong now.

One crushed dream wasn't enough for David.

Her singing dreams were already in tatters. Now he'd taken her job — and with it, her last hope of travelling the world.

She walked out of the office with nothing. No box of belongings. No goodbye. Just a stern face and a silence that dared anyone to speak.

Eyes followed her, but no one said a word.

In the car, the facade cracked. First a few tears. Then a scream. Then more tears — the kind that left her breathless and aching.

She didn't go straight home.

She couldn't.

Her chest was tight, her thoughts too loud, and the idea of sitting alone in her townhouse felt unbearable.

So she drove.

Monique took a detour through the city, rage-singing along to **"Left Outside Alone" by Anastacia**.

By chance—or maybe not—her route led her past the Cyder Lounge.

Maybe she could grovel to Sammy, ask for her singing gig back. Just enough to make some money while she hunted for a full-time job.

She'd find a way to avoid David.

Then again, maybe he was at the Cyder Lounge too, hiding out from the barrage of calls that had flooded his house all day.

But as her car turned the corner, she froze.

The elegant façade was defaced with graffiti. The shop windows — smashed. *Oh no!*

She pulled into a metered spot up the road and jumped out, heart pounding.

The damage looked fresh. The glass and debris had already been cleared, but the place was still a wreck. She broke into a run.

Then she saw him.

David. Standing in the shadows of the ruined entrance, his eyes locked on hers like a heat-seeking missile.

He stepped forward, his expression unreadable — but his jaw was set, and his stride was all fury.

"Come to see the damage up close for yourself, have you?" David spat out.

"What are you talking about? What happened? Oh my god David, is Sammy okay?"

"No, he's not. He's having a mental breakdown over this. I sent him home so me and the crew could clean up the best we can. Now. I know you wanted to get back at me. But taking your anger out on The Cyder Lounge? On Sammy? Well, that's real low Mon."

Monique blinked. Her breath caught in her throat.

"Wait...You think *I* was responsible for this?"

David didn't flinch. "You probably roped one of your exes in to help you. Shane perhaps? He already had beef with me too. It makes sense."

Monique stared at him, stunned. 'Do you really think I'm that kind of person David? Her voice rose. "And you're one to talk. I just lost my job because of you."

His brow furrowed. "You got fired?"

"Yes David." She snapped. 'Because someone reported me for putting a certain number in the survey system more often than it should be. There is only *one* person *that* could be.'

"I did no such thing."

"I don't believe you."

"Well, I don't believe you either."

"Whoa, whoa, whoa — calm down, you two bickering lovebirds." Kyle stepped between them, arms out like a referee. "This little row is cute and all, but we've got work to do."

Monique blinked, grateful. Kyle didn't seem angry with her — which begged the question: if David truly believed she was behind this, why hadn't he told Kyle or Sammy? If anything, Kyle's deathly scowls at David suggested Kyle was pissed off with *him*.

What was that about?

David stood in silence, radiating heat. His jaw was tight, but the fury in his eyes had softened — just slightly.

"I think you should go," David said quietly.

She used to think he saw her clearly. That thought had terrified her — enough to make her run.

Now she wasn't sure he ever had.

Monique didn't bother to respond. She turned and walked back to her car, her heels crunching faint remnants of glass beneath her.

The city noise swallowed her whole.

But her thoughts screamed louder.

She had to walk away. Not because she didn't have more to say — but because staying would mean unravelling. And she'd already lost too much to let him see her fall apart.

Behind her, the shattered windows of The Cyder Lounge reflected the fractured mess they'd both become — two people too stubborn to admit they were hurting, too proud to admit they cared.

David

David, Kyle, and the rest of the Cyder Lounge crew worked late into the night, clearing debris and making calls from the back-office phone — suppliers for doors, windows, carpets, grog, and glasses.

It was a costly venture.

David had taken the reins because his father wasn't coping. The mental load was too much. And besides, this mess was David's fault — it was only right he be the one to try and restore the Cyder Lounge to its former glory.

But as he tallied the quotes just to get the bar back to a bare-minimum operating state, and compared them to their current finances, the numbers didn't add up.

They were in a seriously tight spot.

Why hadn't his father taken out business insurance?

David had no idea the finances were this bad.

With a venue like this, they should've been raking it in.

He'd been blind to what was going on behind the scenes.

The level of detachment he'd had from the place was now painfully, obscenely obvious.

Just as David hung up the phone with the accountant, he spotted a woman loitering near the front of the Cyder Lounge, her shoulders shaking with sobs. He stepped closer.

She looked up, eyes swollen and tear-filled. Recognition hit him like a punch.

Sabrina.

"I'm so, so sorry," she choked out between sobs.

David's stomach turned. He'd slept with her — briefly, messily.

"What happened?" he asked, voice low.

"I told him. Everything," she said, her hand trembling as she tried to cover the bruising around her eye. "But I didn't expect him to do this. I'm so, so sorry."

"Jesus... Sabrina. Tell me what happened."

"He went through my phone. Found the calls and messages. Lost it." Her voice cracked. "He threatened to beat me if I didn't tell him who it was. And when I did... he hit me anyway."

Her sobbing intensified, raw and uncontrollable.

David stepped forward and wrapped an arm around her, trying to steady her shaking frame. The guilt hit hard and fast — heavier than the broken glass still littering the street.

So, Monique didn't do it.

Of course she didn't.

That shit-stain of a human being who hit Sabrina probably rounded up a few goons and sent them here. At least now the police had someone to charge.

As Kyle swooped in, guiding Sabrina inside to call the cops, David stood frozen on the pavement. Guilt and self-loathing churned in his gut — emotions he was becoming far too familiar with lately.

He tilted his face to the sky just as the rain began to fall, soaking his skin and clothes. Each drop felt like a weight, dragging him further down.

Inside, the Cyder Lounge radio — usually set to something upbeat to keep morale going — shifted to a melancholy tune: **"Why Does It Always Rain on Me" by Travis**. Of course it did.

The shattered windows.

The broken trust.

The bruised woman sobbing inside.

Every piece of it traced back to him.

Monique hadn't done this. She never would've. And yet he'd looked her in the eye and accused her anyway. After everything he'd already put her through — trying to win her back, trying to draw her into his bed when he hadn't done the work to deserve her trust.

He'd been so quick to believe the worst of her.

Maybe because it was easier than facing the worst in himself.

The Cyder Lounge would recover—eventually.

But Monique?

He wasn't sure she'd ever let him close enough to fix what he'd broken.

David exhaled, long and low, the cold rain matching the hollow ache inside him.

Should he call her?

No. Not yet.

He didn't deserve that. Not until he did something — something real—to show her he was sorry.

Not just for the accusation. For all of it. For using her. For doubting her.

For being the kind of man she had every reason not to trust.

Chapter 26

Monique

It was day two of unemployment, and Monique was dreading what came next: returning to her old workplace.

In the chaos of her firing, she'd left behind a few things she actually cared about — her pot plant, animal-print notepads and stationery she'd bought with her own money, and most importantly, the photo of her mum pinned to the corkboard beside her desk.

She'd considered leaving it all behind just to avoid the embarrassment.

But eventually, she summoned enough willpower to make it to her front door.

And gasped.

Her handbag slipped from her hand as she stared at the scene beyond the doorway.

The entire front patio had been taken over by troll dolls. Pink, red, yellow, blue, and green—their pointed hair arranged with eerie precision to spell out one word:

SORRY.

This was... unique. She had to give him that.

David must have felt bad — either about her losing her job or finally realising she hadn't been responsible for destroying the Cyder Lounge.

When had he done this?

Her traitorous face twitched toward a smile.

No. This was not cute. Not even close.

It was a pathetic attempt to worm his way back into her good books. And she wasn't having it.

But... that didn't mean she couldn't keep the troll dolls.

After all, this maniacal scheme wasn't their fault.

She gathered them into a plastic shopping bag and tucked them inside before heading off on her dreaded solo mission for the day.

Mid-morning traffic crawled, and Monique's mind spun in loops.

What was she going to do?

She needed a job—desperately. Living alone was expensive, and after the incident, no one in her industry would touch her. Word spread fast.

And who could she use as a reference now?

Certainly not Janice.

She hung her head in shame, wishing she could curl up in her mother's arms and ask for advice—her only true safe space.

But she wasn't safe anymore.

She was alone.

She dreaded walking back into the office to collect the last of her things, and the thought of all those eyes judging her made her stomach turn.

Still, she did what she had to do.

As she opened the door to her old office, she froze.

Julie was sitting behind her desk.

"Oh, hi!" Julie chirped, flashing a confident smile and a sing-song tone.

Monique blinked. "Wait — *you're* team leader now?"

"Yes. *Finally!* I've had my eye on this job for a while now, and it feels *soo* good to be here."

Monique just looked at her, mouth agape until Julie added. "And I am sooo sorry you had to lose your job. Well...not really. But let's be real. You were never supposed to be in this role anyway. You were *never* cut out for it."

Cogs began grinding against Monique's skull, and a lightbulb went off.

"You were the one who told Julie, didn't you. I thought I could trust you. I thought you were my friend."

Julie let out a mocking laugh. "Your *friend*? Really? I only spoke to you occasionally when you first started working here because no one else did and I felt sorry for you. Then when you landed the team leader job, I was a bit pissed off to be honest, until I realised it was probably better to get on your good side. Find a potential weakness to take you down. And I did."

"Why didn't you just tell Janice about my moonlighting gig last year when you found *that* out?"

"I did. But she didn't care. She said whatever you did in your own time was none of her business. Surprising coming from stuck-up Janice and disappointing for me. Lucky I held out though because this outcome was *soo* much better."

Janice walked through the door. "I gave you five minutes to gather what you needed to go. It's now been six."

The cardboard box was already packed, waiting for her to take. She lifted it, casting a sharp glare at Julie and Janice before glancing down. Nestled inside was the beloved photo of her mother—a glamour shot, radiant in her finest, smiling warmly up at her. It felt like a silent reassurance, as if her mother were saying, everything will be okay.

It was fine. *She* would be fine. She didn't need anyone in her life. She was better off alone. Sure, she felt like dumping the pot plant full of soil on Julie's head and telling Janice where to stick it. But she was better than that, so instead of making another decision she would regret, Monique didn't say a word, held her head high and walked out without turning back. It wasn't until she was out the door and back to her car that she let a small tear carve a path down her face, hinting at the well of hurt opening up within her.

A week later, Monique took to the newspapers with her highlighter and pen like a LimeWire user searching for one clean MP3—hopeful, determined, and braced for chaos while singing along to **"Bitch" by Meredith Brooks**.

Looking for a job was tedious: updating her resume, then mailing, faxing, or handing it in to potential employers. It all took time, and all this job hunting did little to help her pay the rent or stop her from dipping into savings.

She had nowhere to be, but the plush leopard-print coat and black lacy cami she wore while completing this menial yet necessary task weren't for anyone else—they were for her. A reminder that she was still fierce, even when the world wasn't watching. There was no audience, no applause, but the outfit helped. It made her feel like she hadn't completely unravelled.

But the truth still stung. She had no one to turn to for help. She was on her own, stuck on a lonely island of her own creation. She'd officially run out of options.

A pull toward the familiar willed her up from the kitchen table and toward the video cabinet, filled with a mix of purchased classics, movies recorded from TV, and home videos.

Monique put the videotape scrawled with 'My Monique First Day of School' in blue biro along the strip of white paper on the front into the VHS player. The black box full of memories was dusty. She hadn't dared look at it since her mother passed away, but a little voice inside her told her today was the day—the day she felt her lowest since her mother had left this world. She didn't think she could handle seeing her mother's face again in motion and colour. Thought it would bring too much hurt and pain flooding back. But right now, she craved the comfort of the familiar—the face and warmth of someone who loved her. Even if it was only pictures made up of pixels on a TV screen.

She still owned the black, brick-sized camcorder too—the one her mother carried with her religiously to capture precious moments with her little girl. She wondered if she'd ever use it to make memories of her own one day.

She was only six years old in this video. Her first day of school. The dark blue uniform freshly ironed. The backpack beside her, full of books and too heavy to carry. She could remember the bundle of nerves she was that day, standing there chewing at her nail, worried about the changes to come. But then her mother came into frame—one of the rare moments her mother joined her on screen, which was exactly why she picked this home video. Usually, she was the one recording memories, but right now Monique desperately wished she was in more of them.

Monique grabbed hold of the nearby velvet cushion and squeezed the life out of it as she let the tears flow—loud, racking sobs, mourning everything she lost when her mother died. Her hope. Her support system. Her positive outlook on the world. Would she ever get it back?

Then she heard footsteps out on the front patio. She looked through the parted Venetian blinds from the couch to see David lurking. Again. Leaving her another gift on her doorstep, probably. The first one—with the troll dolls—was by far the oddest.

A few days ago, it was flowers and a box of Roses chocolates. Both times, he made no attempt to see her. Probably figured that would be a boundary only Monique could give him permission to cross. And sitting here alone, crying over the memory of her mother, she considered crossing it.

She stood up from the couch, wiping tears from her eyes, and opened the door to see David holding a massive gift basket full of decadent treats: chocolate-coated macadamias, gourmet chips and crackers paired with dips and chutneys with fancy names, and so many more treats she couldn't see. Her mouth watered at the sight, temporarily distracting her from her sorrow. But she didn't want David to see that.

"I'll take that," she said matter-of-factly, still sniffing away the tears as she hoisted it out of his arms and into hers.

"Mon... are you okay?" David muttered from behind her, his voice laced with concern as she walked the massive basket of snacks toward the TV.

"I'm sorry. Did you want me to go?"

Monique dropped the basket to the floor with a thud, packets and boxes spilling out. "Come here."

David looked apprehensive, as though she were walking him into a trap, ready to be ripped to shreds. She should punish him. He deserved it. But right now, she needed comfort. As he tentatively walked toward her, she grabbed a packet of crisps and a huge slab of peanut brittle and flopped back onto the couch.

"Sit."

He lowered himself down beside her slowly. Once seated, he looked up to see what she was watching as she hit play on the remote control.

"Is that you, Mon? You are adorable."

Monique couldn't bear to look at him. She just kept watching the screen with her walls up. But it was comforting knowing he was there. Feeling his presence. Someone else was witnessing this precious memory. Not just her.

"And that's your—"

"Mum. Yep, that's my mum..."

Silence stretched between them as she bit chunks out of the brittle, making satisfying crack and crunch sounds.

"Is that your dad behind the camera?"

"No." Monique sucked in air and let out a shuddered breath. "He left my mum when I was six months old. Wasn't cut out to be a dad and had no interest in being in our life. He died in a car crash a year after this."

"Oh," was all David managed to say. But she didn't want him to say anything else. There was nothing else to be said.

This was why her mother was alone. The man who promised to stay with her in sickness and in health had abandoned her when she needed his love and support the most. Her mother had no living family. No friends. It was just the two of them—Monique and Catherine. It was quite sad, really, and she mourned the loneliness her mother must have learned to live with—a loneliness Monique had now come to know all too well.

"You know I could never do that to you. Leave you. I tried and it sucked. I think I'm meant to be here. With you. It feels... right."

"You don't deserve my forgiveness," Monique spat out between sobs, not taking her eyes off the screen.

"I know I don't."

She watched on in silence as her mother fussed over her hair and tied her shoes, telling her things like, "If a kid gives you trouble, tell a teacher. If that doesn't work, punch them," and "Kids can be cruel, so it's best to keep to yourself."

As she watched her mother lead little Monique into school hand in hand—Catherine's grip so tight it appeared she never wanted to let go—Monique realised something. She was raised expecting to be lonely and isolated. Expecting to rely on her mother wholly and completely. Her mother's long-standing wounds had rubbed off on her, and the deliberate attempts to deepen Monique's reliance on her could not be ignored. It was always just the two of them. Catherine and Monique. She was her mother's only friend, support system, and person to turn to in tough times. That was a lot of weight for a little girl to carry.

She was taught not to trust others, but to put up walls. Don't make friends. You're better off alone. And finally, a realisation clicked into place—she didn't want to be lonely and isolated anymore, like her mother was.

She looked across at David, sharing this moment, content in her presence, and she could feel the void that had opened within her since her mother died begin to fill, just a little. The support, comfort, and compassion she needed were right here.

She picked up David's hand from his lap and wrapped it around her shoulder as she leaned into his chest. The weight and warmth of him as he pulled her in closer, stroking her hair, was enough to let the tears flow again. Tears that would release the anguish, the heartbreak, the nothingness.

"My mother," Monique muttered, breaking the silence, her gaze fixed on the now-paused television screen where her childhood self smiled innocently. "She told me, 'Men are temporary. Your dreams are forever.' And she was right. She built me up to be independent, to be a fortress. Just like her. And I get it. She was abandoned by the only man she loved. But because of that, if I admit I need anyone—even for a moment—it feels like I'm betraying everything she taught me."

She paused, taking a ragged breath. "And look at me. I threw away my steady corporate job—my entire financial safety net—for the pettiest revenge plot imaginable. I sacrificed my savings just to sink you. And now my dream of travelling the world feels further away than ever."

David gently cupped her cheek, forcing her to meet his eyes. "I deserved what you did to me, and then some. But you didn't deserve this. You made a human mistake when you were hurting. You lost your job because you were trying to teach me a lesson. The only person who deserves blame here is me, and I'm sorry. For everything."

"But I'm terrified," Monique confessed, the admission costing her dearly.

"I don't have a safety net anymore. If I stop moving forward, if I stop working to secure my future, I feel like I'll sink. Like I'll end up exactly where I told myself I wouldn't be—alone, holding onto a life I never wanted."

David's expression softened, the swagger completely absent. "You are not alone, Monique. You hear me? I won't let you sink."

He reached for her hand, his thumb tracing slow circles across her knuckles. "You deserve those dreams. You deserve the world. And you deserve to chase them. And I won't get in your way."

Monique absorbed his words, recognising the sincerity in his unwavering gaze. This wasn't David the seducer; this was David the supporter. The void she'd carried since her mother's death felt, for the first time, like it was truly beginning to fill.

"We'll figure out the job stuff, together," David assured her. "We'll get you back on a stage that loves you. Because you belong up there. I'm here, Mon. I'm staying."

Monique leaned her head against his shoulder again, this time not seeking refuge from tears, but accepting connection. "Thanks. I think I needed to hear that."

No, David was not perfect. But neither was she. He would need to earn her trust again, but knowing that he was here—and that she would not be alone again—was enough to bring down those walls and let him in, just a little bit.

After some time, pressed against his warmth and listening to his rhythmic heartbeat against her ear, David eventually asked, "So how is job hunting going?"

"Not great..." Monique replied, with no intention of removing herself from his arms just yet.

"Come to the Cyder Lounge with me tomorrow. I'm meeting the old man to sort out our future plans for the place. We'll see if we can get you on the books—maybe get you enough to get by if you don't mind helping us with the cleanup. Until we get the place back up and running and put you back on the stage, that is."

The Cyder Lounge felt like a second home she had run away from. A place where she had felt safe once—and come to think of it, she could feel safe and happy there again.

Monique sat up this time and looked at David. Really looked at him—to see a genuineness and warmth there she had missed and never expected to get back. Could things really go back to the way they were? She didn't know, but she wanted to find a way to get there.

"Sounds good to me."

Chapter 27

David

It was mid-morning on a Tuesday, and David was anxious about meeting his father. He sat at a table in the centre of the Cyder Lounge, the dim interior lit only by warm autumn light filtering through the windows. Monique sat beside him, poised and calm. David was still in shock that she was actually here after everything he'd done. Sure, he'd brought her along to mend things, but honestly, he just felt stronger with her by his side—like he could handle anything as long as she was there.

He had so much to say to Sammy. Sorry for being unreliable and distant. Sorry for taking advantage of his kindness and generosity for so long. Sorry for being the cause of the Cyder Lounge's destruction. Any other father would have disowned him, dropped him on the curb and told him to figure out his own life. But instead, Sammy had smothered him with love—more than enough to make up for the parent he'd lost. And still, it wasn't enough.

The door creaked open and Sammy strode through. Head low. Avoiding eye contact. Sweating profusely. Something was wrong. Just as his father slid into the seat across from him, the door opened again. David's heart leapt into his throat when he saw the woman approaching their table.

"What are *you* doing here?" The words burst out of him.

"Aren't you supposed to say happy Mother's Day?"

May 10th. It *was* Mother's Day.

Sharon Sparks—David's mother, or Sharon Oroque now—arrived with Paul at her elbow, the two of them cutting across the floor like they owned the room. She wore a bright red business suit with oversized gold buttons and shoulder pads, her bleached blonde bob perfectly styled. Paul, the property developer mogul himself, was ten years her senior and borderline obese, his gold chain and watch catching the light from the nearby window. She'd married that twat early last year. They'd gotten an invite to the wedding but of course turned it down.

"Why would I do that?" David shot back. "You're not my mother anymore."

Sharon and Paul slid into the empty seats as if taking possession.

"David. It's been five years. I thought you'd be over this by now."

"I don't think someone ever gets over their mother abandoning them."

"White Noise" by The Living End played softly through the lounge speakers, igniting the rage and hurt swelling within him. He wanted it louder, wanted the music to drown out her words.

"I didn't abandon you. Your father pushed me away. You did too."

"I was a teenager. An angry one because you never fucking cared. And of course Dad pushed you away—you cheated on him!"

Paul pointed a pudgy finger at Samuel. "That man was not worthy of her." He thrust his thumb toward his own chest. "I'm the only man who could give her what she wants."

David glanced at his father, expecting fury. Instead, Sammy's face was creased with worry.

"Plus," Sharon cut in, eyes fixed on David, "you were practically an adult when I left. You didn't need me anymore."

"You left halfway through my senior year. I'd hardly call that an adult. You missed my graduation. I failed all my exams because of you. I have no future because of you."

He yelled it. Screamed it across the room, releasing a truth bottled up for far too long.

Sharon turned up her nose with that smug, holier-than-thou expression that had haunted his childhood. "Well then," she said, voice cold, "Paul and I won't buy this poorly run illusion of a lounge bar, and your father can keep sinking deeper into debt. Ungrateful."

So that's what she was doing here.

"What is she talking about, Dad?"

"Sharon, please. Be reasonable for once." Sammy's voice cracked with desperation. "He's upset. It's understandable after what he's been through—what we've both been through. But I can't afford to keep this place afloat. You won, okay? You won."

Sharon had wanted to keep the Cyder Lounge after their marriage combusted. The deepening rift turned their family into embers for good.

She often talked about the Cyder Lounge being her labour of love, her second child. Beneath the glitzy façade sat her ex-husband's dive bar—the one he'd inherited from his father. She was responsible for turning it into a ritzy establishment. When Sharon moved on with Paul, she hadn't wanted to let it go. She'd tried to keep it and eventually gave up. Now she was back, relishing the chance to reach in and take what she wanted.

Sammy looked small, grovelling at her feet, begging her to save him from financial ruin. And she was relishing every single minute of it. David could see it, and he couldn't stand it.

"After all the work I put into this place." She stroked the nearby wall as if it were a living being worthy of love. "I can't believe you let it fall into such a state."

For a moment, David allowed himself to imagine Sharon was talking about their family, hinting at regret for leaving *them* in ruin. He knew it was wishful thinking—any sign of real concern from her was fantasy. The Cyder Lounge itself felt like proof of the ruin she'd left behind: a tarnished mirror of their family, cracked into pieces that couldn't be fixed. The thought filled him with slow, hot rage.

He could hear his father trying to calmly discuss the terms of transfer. Betrayal tightened around him. Why hadn't Sammy told him this was happening, or that Sharon would be here? He pictured himself walking out rather than watch his father plead, unable to bear the smug satisfaction on her face as Sammy begged to give her exactly what she wanted.

"You can fuck right off if you think you're getting your filthy hands on our bar." David's voice came out low and dangerous, teeth bared.

Sharon turned toward him with slow, mechanical deliberation, as if selecting a new target. Her smile slipped. For a moment, the polished mask cracked.

"I won't be seeing you again if this is how you treat me—like I'm some kind of villain." She rose, voice sharpening. "I am your mother!"

"You are *not* my mother."

If she were really his mother, those words should have stung. He would have seen pain in her eyes. But no. Despite the flaring tensions, her steely glare never wavered. There was no emotion behind those eyes—like a robot programmed to say and do things to suit her own agenda at the expense of those around her. Including her own son.

"Right. I see how it is." Her voice went flat. "I withdraw my offer. Good luck finding a new buyer for this shithole. Don't expect to see me again."

"Sharon! Paul! Wait! No!" Sammy's cry rang with desperation as they both walked out with long, determined strides.

Dread sank in, heavy and slow like blood pooling within him. Whether Sharon bought the Cyder Lounge or not, she would win. Whatever move she made, it was checkmate for them.

Perhaps seeing her ex-husband financially ruined was a greater victory than getting the Cyder Lounge back.

Sammy stood from the table, hands clenched, body tight with frustration as he stormed into the back room. David finally let out a heavy sigh and turned to Monique, who sat quietly beside him. He'd almost forgotten she was there.

"I'm so sorry you had to see that."

She tentatively shifted her chair closer to him, as if preparing for the floor to fall out from beneath them.

David leaned back against his chair, his knuckles white around a half-empty tumbler of whiskey. Monique kicked off her heels, legs curled beneath her like she was trying to shrink away from the chaos that had just unfolded.

The confrontation with his mother had left a crater in the room—emotions scorched, futures uncertain. Samuel Sparks had retreated to the back office, the door shut but not soundproof. David could still hear the occasional thud of frustration, maybe a bottle hitting the desk, maybe just his father's fists against the wood.

Monique broke the silence first, her voice low but clear.

"I get it now."

David turned, his brow furrowed. "What?"

She didn't look at him. Her gaze was fixed on the row of new liquor bottles, their labels glowing like trophies in the dim light.

"I couldn't understand how a mother could be so cold-hearted. Leaving her only son behind, but now I get it."

"Okay, enlighten me."

"She's self-centred. Manipulative. Everything revolves around her and her needs."

David scoffed, the sound bitter. "Yes, I already know all this. I lived with it for 17 years. So?"

Monique turned to him now, her eyes sharp. "So... clearly she's a narcissist."

The word hit him harder than expected. *Narcissist.* It echoed in his mind, bouncing off memories of slammed doors, withheld affection, and the constant ache of being not enough. But the sting wasn't just about her— it was about him. Those same words had been thrown at him before. By friends. By Monique. By himself.

He swallowed hard. "Am I a narcissist?"

"No," Monique said instantly, her voice firm, unwavering. "You care too much. Remember?"

"What does that have to do with anything?"

"Narcissists don't care about anyone else but themselves."

David looked down at his glass, watching the amber liquid swirl. "But you've told me I don't care. About you. About anything."

She sighed, her voice softening. "I was wrong. I guess I tried to make myself believe that to save myself from getting hurt. But you threw a punch and took a punch for me. You remember the things I like. The food I crave. You always greeted me with water and a smile after I walked off stage."

He shook his head. "But everything I touch I fuck up. I'm selfish. I make the wrong decisions. I've failed my dad. I've failed you. I'm just as bad as her."

Monique reached out, placing her hand over his. "Listen to me, David. You are nothing like her. You hear me? Sure, you've been stuck in an illusion of your own grandeur and self-importance for far too long, but clearly you've snapped out of it now."

"Sure. It only took everything around me to go to shit for me to see it."

"Sometimes our world needs to crumble in order to build it back up again into something new."

David looked at her, eyes glassy. "Wise words, Mon. You're too good for me. I don't deserve you."

"I know." She gave a half-smile, then gestured to herself—her dress, her shimmering skin, the perfect makeup. "But all of this is a façade too, you know that right?"

"What do you mean?"

"Fake it till you make it. It's kind of my motto."

"I don't understand."

"This is a costume. The one I wear to become the lounge singer I need to be. Then there's my corporate costume. None of it is the real me. I have to pretend to be someone else to do what I have to do to get what I want. Hence, fake it till you make it, baby."

David leaned back, letting her words settle. He thought about the version of himself he wore like armour around his mates—the bravado, the recklessness. Then the version he became around Monique—quieter, rawer.

"Now wait a minute. You are not faking anything up there on stage. That's the real you shining through. And don't discredit your talent and hard work. You deserve to be on that stage. Deserve to be in that job."

"Oh, I know that. I just don't want to fool you into thinking this version of me is who I am. Because it's not."

David turned to her, his voice low but steady. "Monique. I haven't been pursuing the woman who wears high heels, sexy dresses, and pretends she's tougher than she looks. I've been craving the one who downs a burrito like a champion, puts me in my place when I'm out of line, doesn't take shit from anyone but feels deeply even though she doesn't like to let it show. Sure, she looks great dolled up, but I find her wildly more attractive with messy bed hair and no makeup on. I like to make her smile. And when she does smile for me, it's a genuine one that no one else sees. Only I see that smile, and it's the most addictive thing in the world. I crave it. And I really hope I get to see it again. Even if I don't deserve it."

Monique didn't respond right away. Instead, she reached for his glass, took a sip, and placed it back down. Then she smiled—just for him.

Perhaps they were both pretending—to fit into this world, to be who they thought the world wanted them to be.

But David realised they settled into the truest version of themselves together, in quiet, tender moments like this one, when the world wasn't watching.

Chapter 28

David

Sammy emerged from the shadows of the back room—his body looser, eyes more reflective. As he approached, Monique slipped away, claiming she needed to go for a walk to get some air. David suspected she sensed they needed space to talk.

Sammy sat down across from him, tentative. David paused, inhaled deeply, then exhaled—steadying himself for what he was about to say.

"Why did you let Sharon waltz in here like she owned the place? Like she was entitled to *your* bar?"

There was no sugar-coating it. He needed answers.

"She's not taking it," Sammy said. "I'm selling it to her. Or I was—until you went and ruined the deal."

"I don't understand."

"It's not my bar anymore, David. The Cyder Lounge was your mother's creation. I held onto it because we needed the money. It kept us afloat. Gave you the life I wanted for you. But I'm done with it. And you should be too."

"But the dive bar—you inherited it from your father. It's a family heirloom."

"That's how I justified keeping it. But the bar I inherited is gone. It's something else now, and I don't want to be part of it."

David let the idea settle. The Cyder Lounge had always been part of his life.

Imagining it gone was strange—liberating, even. A feeling he never expected to understand.

"This place is toxic for us, David," Sammy continued. "I know you feel it too. We don't belong here. I'm sorry it took me this long to see it."

David knew exactly what Sammy meant. The dread, the rot, the emotional weight of this space. His mother had poured more love into transforming the bar than she ever gave to him or Sammy. Despite all the work Sammy and David put into keeping the place running, they could not scrub the tarnished source of its creation clean.

His dad was right. They had to let it go—even if it meant handing the prize to the devil herself.

"So, what now?" David asked. "You wouldn't walk away unless you had a plan."

"That's my next surprise. Come on—I'll show you."

Sammy led him out the door and up the strip toward Sips and Stories.

"Maggie's place?" David asked, confused.

Inside, Maggie popped up from behind the bar, beaming. "Hey Sammy. Hey David. How'd the chat go?"

"Not how I hoped," Sammy admitted.

"Oh, that's a shame. We'll figure it out." She reached for Sammy's hand and gave it a squeeze, then turned to David. "So... have you told him the other news yet?"

"Told me what?" David's heart braced for another surprise—hopefully not a bad one.

Maggie raised her hand, fingers spread wide.

David squinted. "Okay... I see five fingers. What am I missing?"

"She's showing you the ring, you goose," Sammy chuckled.

"Wait. What? You two are... together? Engaged?"

They were holding hands now—like a real couple. David struggled to find words. "How long?"

"Been a couple for six months now," Maggie said. "He proposed last week over dinner. But the chemistry? It was there from the start." She squeezed his hand and leaned into him. "Did you know that *your father* was deliberately sending Cyder Lounge deliveries to my bar. Just as an excuse for me to come by and see him?"

Sammy's face flushed, eyes sparkling. "Yeah. Well. It worked, didn't it?"

They'd known each other for two years. Maggie had opened Sips and Stories back in January 1998. Had David really been so distant that he missed this? He didn't know how to feel—excited for them, ashamed he hadn't noticed, worried Sammy might get hurt again. But then he saw how they looked at each other—with mutual affection, real love. His parents had never looked at each other like that.

"Okay, wait," David said, holding up a hand. "This still doesn't answer the big money question. You said you had a plan to get out of the Cyder Lounge."

He glanced between them. "The engagement's great news, really—but I don't see how any of this solves our financial mess."

"I'm going into business with Maggie. Right here at Sips and Stories."

Another surprise David didn't see coming. "Oh...."

Now David took in the space properly. He'd always imagined Sips and Stories as a cramped hole-in-the-wall for artsy types who smoked weed and avoided conversation. But he was wrong. Behind the dark oak door and minimalist frontage was a spacious venue—comparable in size to the Cyder Lounge, but with a real stage currently hosting a poetry reading. Upstairs, bookshelves lined the walls, with cozy nooks for reading and conversation.

Sammy explained their vision. Daytime would remain bookish—live readings, literary events. But evenings would shift to music, drinks, and good conversation. Books would still be available upstairs for those who wanted them.

"I heard Monique lost her job," Sammy said. "If she's interested, we'd love to hire her to sing Thursday through Saturday nights."

"She'd love that," David said. "But are you sure it fits the vibe?"

"You'd be hard-pressed to tell me singing isn't storytelling," Sammy replied. "Especially when Monique does it."

He had a point.

David could picture it—Monique performing, then explaining the meaning behind each song. Adding depth. Adding story. It would be perfect.

David looked across at his father; heart filled with pride. The man who had given David everything and more was finally taking life into his own hands. This dream—this new future—was everything Sammy deserved. David wanted it for him. Wanted it for both of them.

"I'm happy for you. Truly." "We'll figure something out with the Cyder Lounge," David said. "We'll make this happen. I'll make sure of it."

Chapter 29

David

A road trip. To the Sunshine Coast. Noosa was the destination. And somehow, David convinced Monique to come with him.

"Shimmer" by Fuel blasted through the car at full pelt when they pulled up to the impressive house, surrounded by lush hinterland and perched on a hill with a perfect view of the crystal-blue sea. Sharon Oroque's house.

A stroke of jealousy licked at him. *This* is what his mother gave them up for. Who wouldn't want to trade in wiping tables and serving drinks for this life? A life of leisure, living in the lap of luxury. Yep, she had it made and although he hated it, and there was no excuse for what she did, a glimmer of understanding hit him in a way it never had before.

"Remember the plan," Monique crooned, balancing a pavlova topped with whipped cream and fresh fruit. She was the mastermind behind this scheme. David just had to execute it.

His mother needed to be love-bombed. Put on a pedestal. Her narcissism fed with a healthy dose of her own exceptionalism and dominance. And David would deliver it on a silver platter—to get his father the out he needed. A new life. With a woman who gave him the love he deserved.

David rang the doorbell, prosecco in one hand, white lilies in the other.

"Well, well... you came bearing gifts? That's a surprise. Come in."

The ornate double doors opened to reveal white marble floors and a spotless living space decked out in coral and mint green. As he stepped inside, the details hit him—small, deliberate touches that pulled him back to memories of his mother. Not the woman who raised a family, but the curated version of her now on display. Separate. Detached.

On the entryway table sat a gold pendulum clock encased in glass—the same one he used to stare at while doing homework, its steady swing once the quiet soundtrack of his childhood.

The entryway table had a glass top supported by sculpted swans—Sharon loved swans. The seashell decor was unmistakably hers, too. Coral lamps with clam shell bases, oversized wall art framed in gold, each piece embedded with carefully arranged shells. Starfish, conch shells, and triton shells—some as large as his fist—were placed with deliberate precision throughout the home. It all reminded him of beach trips spent collecting shells along the shore, only for her to hoard them in a decorative tray back home. Once they were in that tray, they were off-limits. They were hers.

Just like this house.

Clearly, Paul had handed her full control when it came to decorating—and she hadn't wasted the opportunity.

She led them through the lounge and onto the back veranda, where they were smacked in the face by unobstructed views of the coastline. Deep blue water lapped the tree-lined shore rimmed with white sand.

To think she'd been living a parallel life here left a bitter taste in his mouth. He swallowed hard.

Monique put the Pavlova on the table as they settled in to have one of the toughest conversations of his life.

"So, Sammy sent you here begging for my forgiveness?" Sharon said. "After all these years, you never once tried to visit me—until today. Because you need something."

Classic Sharon. It was always their fault for not reconnecting, never hers for leaving.

David pushed the feeling down. He had to stay composed.

"Sammy doesn't know we're here. This was my idea. *Our* idea."

"I see. And who is this? Your girlfriend? I don't believe we've been formally introduced."

"My name's Monique. I'm a close friend of David and Sammy. I work at the venue too—as a lounge singer. These guys have done an incredible job running the place in your absence. The clientele pays well. It's packed every night, and I'm sure it'll be back at capacity after the renovation."

Sharon eyed them both with a sceptical scowl.

Sharon pointed a manicured finger at David, "So, you *do* want me to buy the place back from Sammy. Now, why would I want to buy back that place in its current state?"

"That's why we're here. To make you an offer you can't refuse."

Sharon crossed her arms and fixed them with a sceptical stare. "Okay, I'm listening."

"You pay us in advance to purchase the venue. We'll handle the full renovation and cover the costs. We'll restore it to a standard you're happy with. You're welcome to inspect the progress anytime."

Sharon leaned back, her smile widening.

"I have another condition."

"What is it?"

"That you visit me. Here. Twice a year. For my birthday and Christmas."

David was blindsided. Shocked. He loathed this woman for what she'd done to him and his father. And now this?

"I don't understand. I didn't think you wanted anything to do with me."

"You're my only son, David. Of course I want you in my life."

"If that were true, why didn't you come back for me when you left?"

Silence hung in the air like a smokescreen. But David saw it—his words cracked through her façade. Revealed something real. Something true.

"I was... unhappy," she said. "I wasn't a good wife to Sammy. Or a good mother to you. I was never cut out for that kind of life—and I resented it. Working in a dirty dive bar all my adult life? I was above that."

She paused.

"So I insisted on renovating the bar. Your father let me. I know he loved me. He'd do anything to keep me from bolting—because I'd threatened it many times before. So, he gave in. Let me have my passion project. And I poured everything into it. It was my fixation and it became exactly what I imagined. I was proud."

"Then I met Paul. I didn't mean for it to happen, but the chemistry was instant. We clicked. I never had that with your father. Paul was my lifeline out of a world where I felt shackled. I wanted to relax. Be treated like a queen. I was done."

She looked at David, eyes softening.

"And I know I didn't think of you in that decision. It's hard to admit, but it's true. I put my needs above yours. I know how wrong that was. But I was drowning, David. I almost left many times before. I even thought about disappearing without a trace. But instead, Paul found me. And I truly believe I'm where I'm meant to be."

David's heart and mind were at war. He'd only ever heard his father's side. Sammy had leaned on him through heartbreak, and David had absorbed that pain.

Sharon was never the doting mother. She'd often avoided parenting altogether, leaving David to fend for himself. But he never realised how close she'd come to leaving it all behind—how deeply unhappy she'd been.

She was sad. He knew that. But he'd kept going like everything was fine. Until it wasn't.

Hearing her side now—finally—healed something in him. He didn't know if he could forgive her. But he understood her. Understood why she did what she did. And maybe, for her own well-being, this was the best outcome—even if it came at a cost to him and his father.

That thought unsettled him. But it was the truth.

The rage, the hate, the endless swirl of anger inside him quieted. His mind cleared. It was never about his worth. Never about her not wanting him. It was about her mental health. Her inability to cope with the life she'd been tied to.

Knowing that lifted a weight he hadn't realised he was carrying. One that had pressed down on his self-confidence, his self-worth, his outlook on life.

Amazing, really—how a few words from someone who shaped your formative years could crack open so much healing.

So... could he bear to see her again? Be in her life? Could he find forgiveness—not for her, but for himself?

"So how about it?" she asked. "Do you think you could let me into your life again?"

David looked at her. Really looked.

"Yes, Mum. I think so."

Chapter 30

Monique

Seeing those walls break down between David and Sharon felt intimate. Special. A moment too sacred for someone outside of the inner circle to witness. But she got to see it. Their two broken halves coming together over sips of Prosecco and bites of crisp yet marshmallowy pavlova with the sweet tang of passionfruit drizzled on top.

It was the kind of moment that made her chest ache — not from sadness, but from the quiet hope that maybe people could find their way back to each other. Even after years of silence. Even after damage.

Instead of veering off towards the highway back to Brisbane, David turned the car into Caloundra and pulled up in a carpark alongside a sandy stretch of beach.

"What are you doing?"

"You didn't think we'd drive all the way to the Sunshine Coast and not hit the beach, did you? Gotta make the most of the trip."

"I'm not swimming. I don't have a change of clothes."

"Who said anything about swimming? We can just walk along the beach, soak in the sea air and build a sandcastle or some shit."

As they walked the sandy pathway past the coastal vegetation buffer towards the shore, the white sand stretched before them towards a churning blue sea. The wind whipped through Monique's loose hair, forcing her to pull it into a messy ponytail as they walked along the stretch of sand towards some rock pools.

"We could do more of this, you know. Travel. Together. That's the other dream we need to tick off your bucket list, right?"

Monique looked across at him slowly. "Wait. *We?* Is *we* a thing now?"

"I know, it's wild." David shook his head, running fingers through his hair, "I didn't see it coming either. But here we are—and somehow, you've made me want something I never thought I'd be ready for. Being with you... it just feels right. Like I've been kidding myself thinking I could ever want anyone else."

David stepped onto the slick edge of the rockpool. A cocky smile spreading across his face as he offered her his hand. Monique's gaze lingered—tracing the curve of his toned arm before finally landing on those dark, dangerous eyes that always seemed to undo her.

Her cheeks flushed. But instead of taking his hand, she pulled herself up onto the rocky edge beside him, flashing a smirk of her own.

She laughed—soft, cautious. "You're good with words, David. But I've heard them before. I need more than promises. I need something that lasts."

Waves surged over the rocks, sending cool water swirling around her ankles and seeping into the crevices beneath her feet. "I'm not just any girl. I'm *the* girl. I'm special."

"So... you think you're special?"

"If I don't believe I'm special—or at least try to—who else will?"

"I will." David said, quiet and certain, his eye penetrating as though he could see straight into her soul.

That look—the one with just enough mischief to make her heart skip, but anchored by something deeper, something real—never failed to undo her.

The words had slipped from his mouth so easily, like they'd always lived there. Like they weren't a line, but a truth he'd finally stopped running from.

She looked down at a hermit crab circling a patch of water, protected in its shell, isolated from others in its limited space. Vulnerability stung. Her heart was still bruised from the last time David held it too tightly—and let it slip.

"How am I supposed to believe anything you say?" she asked, voice light but firm. "And I can't do real feelings right now. I don't have a job, and I've dropped most of my savings on rent."

He nodded. No protest. No push. Just quiet understanding in his eyes.

"Move in with me, Monique."

"No." Her response came fast. Harsh.

"Why?"

"Because I like my place. My stuff. Plus, I don't trust you yet. Not completely."

The bridge between them was building, no doubt. But she wasn't ready to cross it. Not yet. Too much was still left unsaid.

David stepped cautiously around the rock pools, peering into the puddles.

"Kyle moved out," he said. "It's just me now. And I don't like it much. Living alone."

"I see."

Monique stood before the same rockpool, staring at the same hermit crab. The only living creature she could find among the rocks and sand. She thought he was alone—until the sand shifted and another crab emerged. Not alone. Together.

She understood how David felt. She'd lived alone most of her adult life. She'd gotten used to it—the solitude. There was peace in it, sure. But she craved connection. Communication. A feeling of togetherness she'd lost when her mother passed away.

David was the only person she felt that with. Someone she could imagine living with. They were comfortable in each other's presence. Despite everything, she wanted to believe they could fix it.

And rent was killing her.

As she watched the two hermit crabs encircle each other in their quiet dance, Monique found herself saying—

"Move in with *me*."

Splash.

Monique looked up to see David sitting in a rockpool puddle, completely drenched, wiping water from his face and hair. "What did you say?"

She tiptoed carefully around the rocks, offering her hand.

"Live at my place. It's smaller. Cheaper. Plus, I don't have to move or sell any of my stuff. Far more favourable option, don't you think?"

"But it's only one bedroom?" David looked up at her hand, then her face, still unsure.

"Is that going to be a problem?"

David smiled—a broad, genuine smile that made her giddy. He grabbed her hand tight, and she pulled him toward her. As he stood, soaked shirt clinging to his chest, mere inches from her, he muttered, "Not at all."

Monique held his steady gaze. He'd already looked damn good standing there on the beach, sun-kissed and smug. But now—soaked from head to toe, water gliding down his skin—he was downright irresistible. He was her ultimate weakness without a doubt. She's fallen into his trap too many times now for him not to be.

He looked back at her like she was the only source of water in an endless desert. Thirsty and desperate for a taste. She broke eye contact and backed away, still hesitant to quench his desire despite her bold declaration and promise.

"Don't make me regret this."

She hadn't forgotten his betrayal, and she couldn't completely ignore the desire to preserve herself from any more hurt that could come her way despite just giving up her home and her solitary sanctuary to him on a whim.

"You won't. Not this time. I'll earn back your trust—with my immaculate cleaning skills, breakfast in bed, surprise foot rubs, and a guaranteed apology dance if I forget to take the bins out."

Monique rolled her eyes, but she couldn't hold back a smile either. She wanted this. Wanted to believe him this time. But words were only words, and while she had seen plenty of actions recently to prove he'd changed his ways, she'd need more proof to open her heart to him completely.

They stepped off the rocks and onto the warm sand, walking side by side up the beach.

"So," David asked, "are we a *we* now?"

"That depends."

"On what?"

"On you."

David stopped. Turned to face her. Held both her hands between his, gaze piercing and unwavering.

"Monique, I'm sorry. I can't even put into words how sorry I am."

She felt the weight of his gaze—serious, gentle—and the light touch of his hands, his thumbs tracing slow, soothing circles into her palms.

"For what I put you through. For what I put Sarah through. I never meant to be in a relationship with her. She started calling me her boyfriend, and I didn't have the heart to correct her. I just went along with it—too afraid of hurting someone else, too afraid of pushing her away like I did with you."

He stepped closer, his grip tightening just slightly, grounding her in the moment.

"But it got out of hand. It never should've dragged on. And I should never have pursued you while Sarah was still in the picture. I was selfish. Immature. You were right to walk away. I wasn't ready. I didn't deserve you."

"Damn right you didn't," Monique said, brow raised. Her voice held less bite than before—more truth than anger.

She didn't pull away, but she didn't lean in either. The air between them was charged, fragile. She could feel the sincerity in his eyes, but trust wasn't something she handed out easily anymore.

David's voice softened, the bravado stripped away.

"You're above me in every way," he said, his tone low, reverent. "And maybe I still don't deserve you. But I need to try. Because you make my life better, Monique. You make *me* better. And I want to be better. For you."

Monique let the words settle. Then, gently, she pulled her hands from his and turned toward the car, her footsteps slow but steady.

"If it's a relationship you want—with me—don't use me to fill a hole inside yourself," she said, glancing back at him. "You need to fill that on your own. We're two whole people who become stronger together. Not two halves looking for the missing piece. I don't want that. I never want that. I don't depend on others. That's how I get hurt."

David followed, his steps matching hers.

"You're right," he said, no hesitation. "You are your own woman. Strong.

Independent. And I never want to change that. It's what I love most about you."

He reached for her hand again, not to hold her back, but to walk beside her.

"I don't want to take anything away—I just want to build you up. Support you. And I hope you'll do that for me."

They reached the car, the ocean breeze brushing past them like a quiet witness. David opened the door and turned the engine on. The radio playing **"You're Simply the Best" by Jimmy Barnes and Tina Turner.**

"I don't need you to fix me," David continued. "I'm fixing myself. Day by day, I'm healing. Growing. But I can't deny the part you played in helping me get there. If you hadn't come into my life, I'd still be living in an illusion. Drinking away my sorrows. No hope of patching things up with my estranged mother. *You* did that."

Monique kicked at the sand as she walked, her steps lighter now, her heart less burdened.

"I had to," she said softly. "I couldn't bear seeing how much you suffered. I see the change in you. I feel it. And I'm proud of you. I want you to be happy."

David stopped, turning to face her fully. His voice was barely above a whisper.

"You make me happy, Monique. Only you. No one else."

She looked up at him, eyes shining with something new—something brave.

"You too."

Monique's breath caught as David stepped closer, the space between them shrinking to nothing. His eyes searched hers—not for permission, but for truth. And she gave it to him, in the way her gaze softened, in the way her body leaned in without thinking.

The wind curled around them, warm and salty, but all she could feel was him. His presence. His pulse. The way her heart stuttered in her chest as he reached for her cheek, fingers brushing lightly against her skin like he was afraid she might vanish.

She didn't.

She stayed.

And when his lips met hers, it wasn't tentative. It was everything—months of tension, heartbreak, longing, and hope crashing together in one breathless moment. His mouth was warm, sure, and hers responded like it had been waiting for this exact kiss, this exact man, all along.

She gripped his shirt, still damp from the ocean, anchoring herself to the moment. To him. The kiss deepened, slow and hungry, and the world around them blurred into salt air and soft sand and the sound of waves breaking in the distance behind them.

When they finally pulled apart, her forehead rested against his, breath mingling, hearts thudding in sync.

She didn't speak. She didn't need to.

She just smiled—and for the first time in a long time, it felt like the beginning of something real.

Chapter 31

David

As David tugged the damp shirt over his skin, Monique watched him with that quiet, knowing smile—the one that always made his chest ache in the best way. He still couldn't believe it. She'd asked him to live with her. *Live with her.*

What a trip. A wild one—but a good one.

Back on the road with a new, dry fit, he reached across the centre console and laced his fingers through hers. Something so simple, so intimate. He'd never imagined doing that with anyone else. But with Monique, it felt strange *not* to. His hand belonged there. In hers.

Outside, the sky was shifting—brushed with streaks of orange and gold as dusk crept in. The day was slipping away, and with it, the magic of everything they'd just shared. His heart sank at the thought of it ending.

He didn't want it to end. Not yet.

Instead of heading for the highway, David veered off course, steering them into a quiet seaside town just up the coast. There, across from the beach, sat the Barra Pub, a dive bar his father used to love. Said it reminded him of what the Cyder Lounge used to be—before the renovation.

The bar buzzed with warmth—low laughter, clinking glasses, and "**Tip of My Tongue" by Diesel** played on the speakers just loud enough to enjoy while socialising. The floorboards creaked underfoot, the walls wore their age proudly, and the air smelled faintly of salt and spilt beer. A chalkboard menu hung crooked above the counter, boasting cheap drinks and no-nonsense specials. No frills. No performance. Just comfort.

David stepped inside hand-in-hand with Monique, her fingers laced through his like they'd always belonged there. The crowd parted just enough for them to pass, and for a moment, the noise faded into the background.

His chest swelled with something he hadn't felt in years—peace, maybe. Or joy. Or the quiet thrill of being exactly where he was meant to be.

This was what he'd been running from? Commitment, connection, the kind of love that didn't demand perfection. He felt like a fool for ever thinking anything else could compare.

She'd given him another shot. When he hadn't earned it. When he'd broken things that should've stayed whole. And yet, here she was—beside him, choosing him.

He squeezed her hand a little tighter, grateful in a way words couldn't express.

"Champagne for me," Monique said.

"Iced water," David added.

She arched a brow. "Well, haven't the tables turned?"

"Life is good. Don't need that addiction dragging me down. And you're drinking now? How come?"

"It's just one of life's little pleasures I didn't allow myself to have until now."

"Why?"

"I realised I tied a lot of my own insecurities and fears to it. Insecure about losing control while under the influence and allowing my composed mask to slip. Afraid I could wind up addicted to it like my father was—A factor that contributed to his death—drink driving. But I know my limits. A drink or two on occasion isn't harmful. In fact, it's really wonderful, actually."

David wrapped his arm around her and kissed Monique on the cheek; his heart filled with pride and adoration.

"You are incredible. You know that?" Now, if there was anything David could get addicted to, it was the way this drop-dead gorgeous woman looked at him. Like he was someone worthy of love. And that look and everything contained within it was enough to shatter his world and reform it anew.

Monique was tucked against his side, radiant and relaxed, her champagne flute catching the light as they weaved through the crowd. He couldn't stop smiling. This was what he'd been running from—commitment, vulnerability, real love—and now that he'd stopped running, he felt like a man reborn.

Monique leaned into him, and he let his hand rest on her hip, grounding himself in the present. Then suddenly, he felt the tension shift in the room. Something was off. He glanced back just in time to see a familiar face rise from his seat, eyes locked on him with a fury that made David's blood run cold.

Before he could react, the guy was in front of him, shoving through the crowd like a man possessed. David barely registered the movement before a fist connected with his jaw, sending him stumbling backward.

"What the hell, bro?" he barked, clutching his face, stunned.

The crazed man grabbed his shirt, dragging him close. David could smell the beer on his breath, see the wild desperation in his eyes. "Where is Sarah?" He demanded, voice low and dangerous.

David blinked. "What are you talking about?"

"Sarah. Your girlfriend. Who's in love with you!"

Oh. So that's what this was about. David's mind clicked into place, and he couldn't help the laugh that escaped him. "Oh, I know you. You're Sarah's weird uni friend. Newsflash, buddy—Sarah dumped my ass three months ago."

Michael reeled like he'd been gut-punched. "What?"

"She said she had met someone new, though I reckon she just got sick of my shit." David shrugged out of Michael's grip. "Personally, I'm glad to put that whole drama behind me. I'm a different man now."

Monique stepped in, ever the diplomat. "I'll make him send Sarah a huge 'I'm sorry' gift basket for what he put that poor girl through, and I'm sorry for the part I played in that mess too."

David glanced at her, heart swelling with the weight of everything she'd endured. He had hurt her—been the reason it all fell apart. And yet, she'd become the very force that helped him rebuild. Somehow, she'd stayed. She'd forgiven. And he was a better man because of it.

"And don't you feel bad about punching him—he deserved it," Monique added with a playful scowl, giving David a light jab in the shoulder.

"I made him pay for what he did, too. But despite everything I put him through, I still couldn't shake him."

David shrugged, eyes never leaving hers. "Monique is and always has been the woman for me. Just needed to be dragged through some deep shit to see it and appreciate it." He pulled her in, kissed her forehead, and held her like she was the only thing anchoring him to the earth.

Behind them, Michael stood frozen, his expression unreadable. David didn't look back. He'd made peace with the past. He had no idea what Michael was thinking, but he hoped—genuinely hoped—that the guy would find his own version of this. Of her. Perhaps in Sarah. Because she deserved to be loved like this, too. Maybe more than anyone.

Because once you've fallen, really fallen, you don't just get back up. You learn to live differently.

Monique

David's hand enveloped hers across the centre console, sending a current through Monique's veins as **"It Feels so Good' by Sonique** played through the car speakers, the lyrics and vibe lighting a fire within her.

She stole a glance at him—treacherous, infuriating, *devastatingly* handsome—and her pulse quickened. With her free hand, she traced the inside of his arm with her manicured nails, dragging them upward, over the taut curve of his bicep, until his skin prickled beneath her touch. A shiver ran through him, subtle but unmistakable.

His jaw tightened as he steered the car onto a winding coastal track, the road climbing higher, tighter, until the world opened up before them. The lookout sprawled beneath a sky so vast it made her breath catch—a canvas of stars bleeding into the endless black of the sea below. The waves crashed against the rocks in violent, frothing bursts, the salt-tanged wind whipping through the open windows.

Two other cars idled in the distance, silhouettes of people lingering near the edge, but David pulled away from them, parking in the shadows where the darkness could swallow them whole.

The engine died. The silence that followed was thick, charged. His gaze locked onto hers, heavy with hunger, before he leaned over her, his fingers deftly unbuckling her seatbelt. Then his mouth was on hers—hard, demanding, possessive—his arms banding around her. The taste of him, the heat, the way his body molded to hers—it was intoxicating.

She broke the kiss just long enough to breathe, "I thought we were here to admire the view."

His lips curved against her throat. "I already am."

Before she could react, he was already out of the car, circling to her side. He offered his hand, steady and insistent, guiding her out. The wind struck first—hair lifting, salt air engulfing her senses. As she moved to the front of the skyline, David's gaze locked on hers. In one swift, hungry motion, he pressed her against the hood, the cool metal biting through the thin fabric of her skirt. He loomed over her, a dark silhouette framed by the churning sea and the endless sky, the wind tangling her hair as his body pinned hers. His kiss was a storm—ravaging, relentless—his hands roaming, claiming, until she was nothing but sensation.

Then he flipped her, chest to the hood, her short skirt riding up, the night air cool against her exposed skin. His fingers hooked into the delicate lace of her G-string, tugging it aside before he pressed into her—slow, deliberate, *filling* her completely. A shared groan tore from them, raw and guttural.

She *should* have cared that someone might see. That the other cars were still there, that the wind carried the sound of her gasps, that the sea below was a witness to their sin. But the thrill of it—the forbidden, the danger, the way his body moved inside hers—sent her spiralling. The salt on the air, the crash of the waves, the stars burning above them—it was too much, too perfect, and she never wanted it to end.

His hands gripped her hips, fingers digging in as he drove into her—harder, faster—each thrust pushing her closer to the edge. Then he flipped her again, her back against the hood now, her cami yanked down to expose her breasts. His mouth closed around her nipple, wet and hot, his other hand fisting in her hair as he buried himself deeper, his rhythm punishing.

His lips found her ear, his breath ragged. "You're so fucking sexy."

The words sent a jolt through her, and she arched into him, her nails raking down his back. He responded with a growl, his pace brutal, relentless—until headlights sliced through the darkness.

A car crept toward them, searching for the perfect view.

David stilled, his body tensing, but Monique twisted her head, her voice a low, desperate command. "Keep going."

Something dark and feral flickered in his gaze—his jaw set, his breath coming faster. He wasn't just a man anymore; he was *hers*, and she would have all of him, consequences be damned.

With a rough grip, he flipped her back onto her stomach, the new angle letting him sink even deeper. His fingers found her clit, circling in slow, maddening strokes as he pounded into her, the car's headlights now close enough to illuminate them—two bodies tangled in sin, the hood of the car groaning beneath them.

Monique didn't care. The risk only made it hotter, the spotlight of the headlights like a match to kindling. Her toes curled, her back arched, and then—

Pleasure exploded through her, a deep, shuddering moan ripped from her throat as her body convulsed around him. She went boneless, her weight collapsing against the car, her legs trembling, barely able to hold her up.

A car door slammed. "You are disgusting. I'm calling the cops."

Monique barely had time to register the voice before David scooped her into his arms, laying her across the backseat with a care that contradicted the roughness of moments before. He pressed a quick, possessive kiss to her lips, then slid into the driver's seat, peeling away from the lookout with a roar of the engine.

Laughter bubbled up in Monique's chest, breathless and giddy. David's own chuckle joined hers, low and dark.

She couldn't think of a better way to end the night.

Chapter 32

David

Four weeks after the destruction of the Cyder Lounge, Sammy and David hesitantly re-opened the doors, despite the renovations still being underway. Once the essentials were in place and any major hazards were taken care of, they needed patrons through the door to start making money again. Two more months left of renovating the place and sorting out all the transfer paperwork and the Cyder Lounge would officially be out of their hands.

Despite the bar being open, it did not yet resemble the glamour their patrons once knew with mismatched furniture, a tarp over the broken window that was being repaired next week, and regulars sipping beer amid the chaos.

The only real drawcard they had was Monique—willing to sing every night, just to keep the doors open and the crowd coming back. She very quickly became the heartbeat of the place again. He admired her from behind the bar, as he always did on nights she performed. Up on stage in her maroon snakeskin halter-neck dress and black choker with a silver heart at its centre, she sang her own rendition of **"Say You'll Be There" by the Spice Girls** with the kind of raw conviction that made the entire room look at her and pay attention.

David, meanwhile, decided it was time to stop coasting. He enrolled to finish the Diploma of Hospitality Management at TAFE, determined to finally earn a qualification and build something solid. Juggling classes, study, bar shifts, and the ongoing renovations was relentless. Full-on. But worth it.

Worth it to see his old man look at him with pride, perhaps for the first time in his adult life.

Worth it to feel, for the first time in years, like he was working toward something real.

He was busier than he'd ever been—exhausted, stretched thin, worn down in body and mind. But strangely, he'd never felt more alive. Every ache had purpose. Every late night meant progress.

And in the middle of it all, Monique.

Her voice. Her fire. Her belief in him.

He was building something. Not just skills. Not just a future.

He was building himself.

David was mid-pour behind the bar when he looked up and spotted Sharon. That red business suit—five years past fashionable—made her impossible to miss, along with the oversized clip-on earrings and a chorus of gold bangles jangling at her wrists. Her scowl deepened as her eyes swept over the half-finished chaos around her.

Beside him, Sammy let out a tortured sigh. "Here we go," he muttered, circling the bar to intercept her.

David offered a polite nod, then busied himself with polishing an already spotless glass, feigning focus while straining to catch every word of the conversation about to unfold.

Sharon looked like she'd just opened her mobile bill after a month of international roaming —arms crossed, mouth puckered tight. "This is a disgrace," she snapped. "I can't believe you'd open the place in this state. If it's not up to scratch by the deadline in the contract..."

"It will be ready, Sharon." Sammy cut in. "The reno costs have been adding up. We needed to open the doors to fully fund the new fit-out."

"Or fund your upcoming wedding?"

"Sharon..."

Sharon's expression softened, arms loose to her sides, "Despite what you may think of me, I'm not a heartless witch. Truly. I am happy for you, Sam. I know we haven't seen eye-to-eye. But you're a good man. You weren't the right man for me, but hopefully you will be for her, and she will be for you in return."

"Thank you." Sammy sucked in a deep breath, "And I'm sorry for ignoring the invite to your wedding with Paul. I was still hurt. Wasn't ready. I handled the split poorly too, and I apologise."

Sharon held out a hand for a handshake. Her way of offering an olive branch. A truce in the bitter feud between them finally broken. Sammy took it, offering a small but sincere smile in return.

David stood behind the bar watching, silently admiring. This was a moment he never anticipated. He had found some closure, but his father needed it too—so he could fully embrace his new future with Maggie.

David stood behind the bar, hands idle, heart quietly thudding. He watched them—his parents—leaning in, speaking softly, the tension between them finally beginning to melt. It was a moment he hadn't dared to imagine. He'd made his peace months ago, stitched together his own version of closure. But his father had been slower, still carrying the weight of unfinished conversations and old regrets. Now, with Maggie waiting in the wings and a new chapter calling, *this* was the release *he* needed. David blinked, swallowed, and let the sight settle deep in his chest like a balm he hadn't known he was craving.

"Now this place though," Sharon said, gesturing broadly at the half-finished interior. "Gotta get it up to scratch, Sammy, or we're going to have some issues."

And just like that—like a switch flipped—the scowl returned. Bitter. Precise. Regal in its cruelty, like the Queen of Hearts ready to shout *off with their heads* if the curtains weren't hemmed just so. Sammy dipped his head with a tight-lipped smile, the kind that said I hear you. Sharon spun on her heel, gold bangles chiming like warning bells as she strode out the door.

David didn't flinch. She hadn't acknowledged him—barely a glance in his direction—and that was fine. That was Sharon. She wouldn't change. And somehow, over time, David had learned to accept her exactly as she was. More importantly, he'd learned to separate her sharp edges from his own sense of worth. That was his quiet victory.

David shook his head and glanced across the bar at Kyle, hoping to catch his reaction to the whiplash exchange between his parents. Surely he'd seen it—but Kyle didn't meet his gaze. Just turned away, busying himself with something that didn't need doing.

Things had been strained between them ever since David moved out. Their conversations were clipped, limited to bar logistics and essential updates. No jokes, no late-night banter. Just the quiet hum of unresolved tension. They'd all been so consumed with reopening the bar that no one had dared to address the elephant in the room. And David felt it—an invisible wall between them, solid and cold, every time they were in the same space.

He didn't even know where to begin. How do you rewind a friendship to square one when it had been fractured for so long?

So instead of trying, he looked up at the stage.

Monique stood bathed in soft light, commanding the room with every note. A temptress, yes—but it wasn't just her voice that cast the spell. Everyone fell for the performance. But David? He'd fallen for her.

This was love. No doubt about it.

And tonight, he planned to tell her.

Monique

Monique stepped off the stage, heart still thudding from the final note. The applause had faded, but the adrenaline lingered. Sammy was waiting near the bar, grinning like a proud uncle.

"Monique, darling," he said, pulling her into a quick hug. "There's someone here who'd love to meet you."

She followed his gaze to a sharply dressed man in his sixties, silver hair slicked back, eyes bright with intent. He stepped forward, extending a hand.

"You are exactly what I've been looking for," he said. "That voice. That look. It's perfection."

Monique blinked. "Why thank you... looking for what, exactly?"

"Let me introduce myself. Larry Walters. Chief Entertainment Officer at Paradise Cruises."

Her breath caught.

"I've been searching for the perfect lounge singer to perform on our luxury cruise lines," he continued. "And you, Monique, are exactly what we need."

"Really?" she said, trying to keep her voice steady.

"Yes, really. How would you like to be paid to live and perform while traveling the world on our ships?"

Fireworks exploded in her chest. Singing and travelling? Her two greatest dreams, bundled into one impossible offer. Surely there was a catch. This sort of thing didn't happen to people like her.

She glanced toward the bar instinctively—toward David—but he was gone. Sammy followed her gaze.

"He had to duck out," Sammy said quietly. "Picking up a delivery."

Right. Of course.

Larry was still watching her, waiting for a response. She scrambled for words.

"Yes," she said, breathless. "That sounds amazing. Thank you!"

But then the weight of reality crept in. Her excitement faltered.

"Wait... I'm not sure if I can," she added, voice dipping. "I mean, I have commitments." She turned to Sammy. "What about Sips and Stories?"

"Don't you worry about that. This is your dream darling. Take it!"

Larry smiled, patient. "Of course. Take time to think it over. But I'll be honest—we'd love to have you. And we move quickly. If you're interested, we'd need to start the paperwork within the week."

She nodded, mind spinning. Sammy gave her a gentle nudge.

"Go talk to him," he said. "Figure out the details. I'll cover the bar."

The meeting with Larry took place in a quiet booth tucked away from the crowd. He laid out the offer in crisp, confident terms: an extendable six-month contract aboard the Pacific Sun, starting December 1st, just in time for the summer holiday season. The ship would sail through Vanuatu, Fiji, Samoa, Papua New Guinea. Later, she could transfer to other liners—New Zealand, Hawaii, maybe even global routes.

It was everything she'd dreamed of. Everything her mother used to talk about when they'd sit on the balcony and imagine a life beyond Brisbane.

And yet, as she signed the preliminary paperwork and shook Larry's hand, a knot formed in her stomach.

David didn't know.

She'd wanted to tell him first. To sit him down, explain everything, reassure him that this wasn't about leaving *him*, but about finally stepping into the life she'd been building since grief cracked her open.

But now the moment had passed. He'd missed it. And she'd said yes.

As she walked back toward the bar, contract tucked into her bag, the candlelight from the stage still flickering in her mind, she felt the full weight of it.

Excitement surged through her veins. This was happening. She was going to sing across the Pacific.

But dread curled around the edges of her joy.

She had to tell David.

And she had no idea how he'd take it.

Chapter 33

David

David watched Monique step through the front door of her home—*their* home now— as **"Kiss from a Rose" by Seal** played, and his heart did that stupid flutter thing again. She paused, blinking at the flickering glow that filled the room. Candles. Everywhere. He'd gone full rom-com cliché, because according to every soppy movie he'd ever half-watched, dim candlelight meant romance.

Fire hazard? Probably. But he wanted tonight to feel special.

The dining table was set with a roast lamb feast—crispy vegetables, a jug of gravy, mint sauce, and a tray of Yorkshire puddings that had collapsed into sad little craters the moment he pulled them from the oven. He'd stared at them for a full minute, wondering if he should bin them. But no. He'd made them. They stayed.

"Well, isn't this a bit romantic." Monique said, her voice warm with amusement.

"What can I say?" he replied, stepping forward with a grin. "I'm a man who's eager to please."

Monique settled into her seat across the table, candlelight flickering against her skin. She looked radiant—relaxed, curious, and completely unaware of the emotional grenade he was about to toss into the room.

Monique picked up her fork, then paused, eyes dancing with mischief.

"Did Sammy tell you?"

David blinked. "Tell me what?"

"My big news!"

"No..."

She tilted her head, playful. "Oh wait—did *you* have big news for *me* too? Is that what this is all about?"

"Well... yeah, I guess you could say that."

Her grin widened. "Well, that's a bit fun. I guarantee my surprise is better than yours."

"I doubt it."

"Okay. Let's do it this way. I'll count us in—three, two, one—and we say our surprises at the same time."

David's pulse kicked up. This wasn't how he'd planned to say it. Actually, he hadn't planned much beyond the dinner. But now, the moment was here—served up on a silver platter. Her big news was going to sound so trivial, he thought, announcing a new troll doll collectible or gossip from a co-worker at the Cyder Lounge, compared to *his* earth-shattering confession.

"Okay, let's do it," he said.

Monique raised her hand like a conductor. "Three, two, one..."

"I'm going overseas," she said.

"I love you," he said.

Silence.

It stretched between them like a pit. He stared at her, stunned, as if the air had been sucked out of the room.

Overseas?

She's leaving?

How? When?

"I got a job," she said, voice soft but steady. "On a cruise ship. As a lounge singer."

"So... overseas for good then? Not just a holiday?"

"Yep."

His confession shrank in the shadow of hers. The words he'd been holding onto for weeks—months—now felt small. Drowned out.

"That's amazing news," he said, forcing a smile. "Exactly what you wanted, right?"

"David…"

"Singing and travelling? Wow. Both dreams wrapped up in one. Congratulations."

"Thank you, but David… you just said you love me."

"Yeah. No big deal."

Her brows lifted. "That's a *huge* deal. I—"

"No, no. Your news is way bigger than mine. I mean, how could I compete with that? All your dreams coming true. It's bloody excellent."

"It is. I'm excited. And nervous."

"Mon, you're going to crush it. Kill it. It's an incredible opportunity."

"You really think so?"

"I know so, babe. You're made for that job. And I'm so damn proud."

And he was. Proud. Of everything she'd fought for. Everything she'd become.

But happy? No. He couldn't say that. Not when this meant losing her. Not when she'd be gone—out of reach, out of their shared rhythm, out of *his* life.

She wouldn't be his. They wouldn't be *them*.

He'd be left floating again, untethered. No anchor. No Monique.

But he refused to dwell on that. Not tonight.

This was her moment. Her triumph. And he would lift her up, bask her in the glow of it, even if his own confession faded quietly into the background.

Chapter 34

David

David sprawled across the bed, face buried in a pillow that smelled faintly of roses—of Monique's perfume while listening to **"Not a Day Goes By" by Rick Price** on the stereo. Her scent lingered in the fabric, soft and familiar. This was her bedroom—or as he cheekily called it, her "boudoir."

Technically, they shared the space now, but his clothes were still packed in suitcases, his belongings confined to a set of drawers in the corner. He felt like a guest. A temporary resident. Because that's what he was.

In a few short months, Monique would be gone. Sailing the seven seas—without him.

She was destined for bigger things, and he knew it. But that didn't mean he was ready to let go.

David gazed up at Monique's collage hanging on the wall, framed and complete—the one she credited for making her singing and travelling dreams come true. But the "Fake it till you make it" phrase in the centre, spelled out with magazine letter cutouts, had a makeover. It now said, "Dreams do come true," with the addition of a cut-out photograph of the two of them stuck right in the centre.

It was a beautiful sentiment—including him on her dream board—but he couldn't help noticing how minuscule he looked amongst the other busy and overbearing cutouts around him. His heart sank even further at the thought.

To distract himself from the heartbreak he could already feel creeping in, David threw himself back into his studies. Books and pens were scattered across the mattress like confetti. For some reason, desks felt too rigid. Too formal. Something about lying stomach-down on the bed, pen in hand, kicked his brain into gear.

He was more determined than ever to finish his Diploma of Hospitality Management and finally earn a qualification. His aversion to academics had always been rooted in that final year of high school—when everything fell apart, and so did his grades. His mother's abandonment had branded him with failure, whispering that he wasn't good enough, that study wasn't for him.

But Monique's drive lit something in him. Watching her chase her dreams made him want to carve out his own. Maybe he could be more than the guy who coasted through life. Maybe he could be someone worth staying for. But it was wishful thinking, and he knew it.

Looking around the room, he had to admit to himself that living with Monique was an adjustment. Her décor was a kaleidoscope of animal print, gold, velvet, and cosmic-inspired ornaments. Feature walls sponged by hand—inspired by her favourite home reno show, *Changing Rooms*—were supposed to add texture and flair, apparently. It was chaotic, bold, and unapologetically her. The polar opposite of the barely furnished bachelor pad he had lived in.

He could live with what this place had to offer because of the amazing woman in it. Except for that leather-studded couch. Too damn uncomfortable. Another reason why he was hiding out in the bedroom—but it wasn't the only reason.

Ding-dong.

David threw the pillow over his head, trying—and failing—to hide beneath it.

"It's time."

He looked up to see Monique poking her head into the room.

"Do I have to?"

"Yes."

"Are you sure?"

"Absolutely."

"Fine…"

David pulled himself off the bed, gathered up his study stuff, and put it on the table before walking slowly toward the door, dreading what was on the other side.

Monique nudged him toward it—it was his apology dinner, after all. Time to clear the air with Kyle.

David swung the door wide, flashing a smile that must have looked as awkward as it felt.

"Hi Kyle, Cara. Come on in," David managed to say as Kyle stepped through the door with two six-packs of Tooheys New, followed by Cara, carrying a Tupperware box full of handmade brownies.

They exchanged surface-level pleasantries—footy scores, traffic complaints—until the food was laid out and the air thickened with expectation.

"Okay. Spill," Kyle said, settling into the dining chair fronted with an El Paso build-your-own taco kit that Monique had laid on the table moments earlier—crunchy taco shells, salad, meat, and salsa—because David knew how much Kyle loved tacos. "You don't call me out of the blue and invite me over for tacos for nothing. So, let's clear the air. Don't leave me hanging."

David took a breath as he scooped seasoned mince into his taco shell.

"I should probably start with apologising. To both of you. Kyle—for treating you like shit and acting like I didn't care when you moved out. I did. And Cara—I really messed up our first meeting. I'm sorry."

Kyle nodded slowly as he began to build a taco of his own.

"I appreciate that, man. But I need to know why. Why did you push me away like that? Especially after everything we've been through?"

David hesitated, putting his taco and utensils down to focus on what he had to say.

"I thought I was better than you. That you were jealous of me—my mates, my laid-back life."

Kyle scoffed. "Mate…"

"I know. Ridiculous, right? Truth is, I was jealous of you. My studies got derailed straight out of high school, thanks to my mum. I've felt like I've been playing catch-up ever since. And here you are, about to graduate law. I couldn't handle it. So I pushed you away. I'm sorry I never said it before, but I'm proud of you, bro. I really am."

Kyle's expression softened.

"I knew you'd come around eventually. Thanks, mate. That means a lot."

Kyle leaned forward, his voice dropping to something quieter, more raw.

"In all honesty... I looked up to you, David. Especially in high school. You were like a big brother to me. I wanted to be like you."

He paused, eyes flicking down to his overflowing taco for a moment before meeting David's again.

"But when Sharon left... watching it break you—it messed me up too. You shut down. Stopped hanging out. It was like you disappeared."

Kyle's jaw tightened, emotion flickering behind his words.

"I didn't move in because your dad told me to. I would have moved in anyway. I didn't want you to go through that alone."

David didn't speak, but Kyle pressed on.

"Even when you started partying and hanging with new mates, I stayed. I wanted to be there for you. And yeah, it sucked that you didn't see that."

Kyle's voice cracked slightly, but he steadied it.

"You're my best friend. You know me better than anyone—and I know you. The real you. And I'm glad I've finally gotten to see him again."

He leaned back, letting the silence settle.

"I missed you, bro."

David swallowed hard. "I missed you too."

David stood slowly, the weight of the moment pressing into his chest. He walked around the table and pulled Kyle into a hug—tight, unspoken, overdue. Their first, after all these years. No jokes. No bravado. Just two mates finally honouring the friendship they shared.

Cara and Monique exchanged warm smiles, their eyes lingering on the two men who had just cracked open years of misunderstanding. It was a rare kind of moment—raw, real, and quietly healing.

David and Kyle settled back into their seats, each taking a sip of beer like punctuation to the conversation. The tension had lifted, replaced by something lighter.

Kyle leaned back, grinning.

"And Monique—congrats on tying this wild one down." He pointed across to David. "I never managed it, but you did. How'd you pull that off?"

Monique smirked.

"Mind games, manipulation, a bit of cold shoulder, and a lot of cold calls. He kept coming back for more. He's a glutton for punishment."

"What can I say?" David shrugged. "I love a good challenge."

"And I hear you got a full-time gig performing on cruise ships now?" Kyle asked. "That's huge!"

Monique beamed.

"Thanks. Yeah, I'm over the moon. It's everything I've ever wanted."

David's heart swelled—and then sank. She was everything he'd ever wanted. But he couldn't compete with that dream. He had no right to stand in her way.

Cara reached into her tote bag and pulled out a small, neatly wrapped box.

"Before we forget," she said, handing it to Monique. "A little something for your big adventure."

Monique blinked, surprised.

"You didn't have to…"

Kyle grinned.

"Open it."

She peeled back the paper to reveal a sleek silver digital camera nestled in its box. Her jaw dropped.

"No way."

"It has a whopping five megapixels," Kyle said proudly. "When you print those photos, it should look so crisp you'll think you were actually there again."

Monique laughed, holding it up like a trophy.

"This is incredible. Thank you so much."

Cara smiled.

"We figured you'd want to capture everything."

A camera. Perfect gift. Why hadn't he thought of that?

"And what do you think, David?" Kyle asked. "How do you feel about it all?"

David gave the answer he always gave.

"I'm so incredibly proud. She deserves it."

Because she did, she deserved that dream. But he didn't deserve her. Her love had always been on loan—borrowed time in the shadow of her ambition. It was only a matter of time.

He glanced at Kyle, who was watching him closely while devouring his dinner. Of course he saw it. The doubt. The ache. The quiet unravelling.

David was tired of being the guy people felt sorry for. He thought he'd moved past that. But this gathering cracked open a new layer of uncertainty. He finally felt settled—with Monique, with his studies, with his future. But in a few short months, the one person who truly got him would be gone.

He didn't want to think about it. But he'd have to. Eventually.

And when he did, he'd need to be ready. For the heartbreak. For the silence. For the future without her.

Chapter 35

David

"Your place or mine?" Monique whispered across the bar as David poured drinks for the last time at the Cyder Lounge.

"Both. But you can't afford me."

"How much are you charging?" she teased.

"If you dance for me, I'll consider giving you a discount."

"I dance for no man."

"What if he begged? On his knees?"

"Okay, settle down boy. I'll offer you *one* free dance—if you let me have my way with you later."

"Let's see how the night plays out, shall we?" David winked, heat rising in his chest. He loved the way she teased and tempted him. It drove him wild in the best ways.

The lounge was packed. Regulars, staff, competitors from along the strip, and close friends had gathered for the final night under Sammy Sparks' reign. The Cyder Lounge—once a humble bar, now a luxury lounge—was about to change hands.

Sharon O'Rourke, Sammy's ex-wife, was here too. Alongside Paul. Polite. Jovial. Sharing space with Sammy and David—a sight David never thought he'd witness again. Sharon and Maggie met face to face for the first time. Maggie's sunny disposition melted Sharon's initial frost into something warmer. Warm enough for a hug. Small, but real.

Then came the clink of a fork against a wine glass. The chatter softened just a touch.

Sammy cleared his throat, tapping his glass again. The room quieted.

"I was just a boy when I first stepped behind the bar at my father's pub. Back then, it smelled like beer and wood polish, and the jukebox played more static than music. But it was home. I learned how to pour a pint before I learned how to drive. I watched my old man charm the regulars, settle disputes, and keep the lights on with nothing but grit and a crooked smile.

Years later, I watched my own son grow up in this place. Different music, different crowd—but the same heartbeat. David, you've poured drinks here, wiped tables, listened to stories, and made your own. Just like I did.

This bar has seen it all—first loves, last calls, heartbreaks, and celebrations. And it's changed. Sharon—credit where it's due—had the vision to turn this old watering hole into something elegant. A lounge. A place people dress up for. And now, she's taking the reins again. After everything we've been through, I'm grateful we found common ground. Handing over my half of the Cyder Lounge wasn't easy. But it was right.

Because I'm starting something new too—with Maggie, and Sips and Stories. A different kind of bar. A different kind of dream.

So tonight, we raise a glass. To the past that shaped us. To the future that calls us. And to the people who make it all worthwhile."

Sammy stood tall, glass raised. "To new beginnings," he called out, voice steady but thick with emotion. Glasses clinked. Laughter rippled. And just like that, the final ties to the Cyder Lounge were cut.

Monique took the mic and sang a sultry, bittersweet rendition of **"Closing Time" by Semisonic**. Her voice wrapped around the room like velvet, stirring memories from every corner of the bar.

Sammy turned to David. "How are you feeling, son?"

David hesitated. "Yeah... I dunno." The words barely scratched the surface. His chest was tight, his thoughts tangled. That speech had cracked something open, and he was still trying to hold it all together.

"I know that look. Uncertainty. A hint of fear, maybe. I get it."

"Everything's changing. Again. I know it's a good change, but yeah—it's a lot."

Sammy let out a heavy sigh and laid a warm hand on his shoulder "It's a lot for me too. Letting go of this place isn't easy. But it's right. I know that now."

"Yeah. I know."

"But my dreams, my path with Maggie and Sips and Stories might not be the right one for you."

David didn't know what to say—because his father was right. He felt like a puzzle piece that never quite clicked into place, always hovering at the edges of other people's lives. He wanted to belong. He tried. But even now, with a clearer mind and the woman he loved beside him, he still felt adrift, like he was reaching for a rope that wasn't there.

"All I ever wanted was to protect you," Sammy said. "To set you on a path toward happiness. Some say I should've been stricter. Maybe I spoiled you. But I did my best. And David—I couldn't be prouder of the man you're becoming."

"Thanks, Dad. That means a lot."

David opened his arms and pulled his old man into a hug—genuine, warm, and lingering. When Sammy finally pulled back, his hands stayed clasped on David's shoulders.

"But I've still got a few tricks up my sleeve. A few strings to pull. Sammy Sparks isn't done spinning magic to help his son reach his full potential."

Before David could reply, Monique stepped in. "Excuse me, Sammy. I believe I owe this man a dance."

She pulled David onto the dance floor, her body flush against his, soft hands around his neck. He didn't know what his father had planned—but right now, all he knew was that the only place he wanted to be was here. In her arms.

Monique

Three months later, Monique stepped onto the small stage at Sips and Stories, adjusting the microphone stand with steady hands. The air was rich with the scent of aged paper and brandy, and the polished wood floors radiated warmth—a far cry from the sleek chill of the Lux lounge, where she'd first found her footing and her voice. She glanced up at the second-floor balconies where bookshelves lined the back walls. No one was reading. Everyone was watching her. This was her final gig in Brisbane, a week before the Pacific Sun sailed on December 1st.

Sammy and Maggie's venue felt like a hug—intimate, serious about books, but with a relaxed nightlife pulse just as Sammy had wanted. The room buzzed with expectation; it was a full house with a blend of old Cyder regulars, newer Sips and Stories patrons and curious newcomers.

She caught David's eye. He was tucked into a corner booth, neck deep in notes and textbooks for his Diploma in Hospitality Management, scattered around him. His final assessment was tomorrow, and he was determined to get top marks. He'd been relentless with his TAFE work lately, steadying himself in a way that looked like growth and perhaps distraction, too. Part of her swelled with pride; part of her felt the weight of what she was about to leave behind.

He's putting himself back together, she thought. Building a future that didn't include her—just as he should. But the ache in her betrayed the pride she should be feeling.

Another thought slid under the first, sharper and quieter: he hadn't said "I love you" again since that dinner months ago. She'd wanted to say it back—so badly it lodged under her ribs—but the cruise loomed, the Pacific Sun pulling her away. Saying it now would turn leaving into a tragedy, not the thrilling new chapter it was meant to be. She held the words in like a mouse caught in a trap—still, silent, already mourning its end.

She adjusted the mic and let the dance tune with a melancholy undertone settle as she closed her set with **"Groovejet (If This Ain't Love)" By Spiller**

& Sofie Ellis-Bextor. She poured bittersweet joy into each note—triumph braided with the ache of impending departure.

When she hit the final note, the room erupted. Monique glanced to David. He slammed his textbook shut and strode toward the stage with a confident, almost theatrical gait.

He reached the platform as she lowered the mic. She expected a private compliment, maybe a whispered request. Instead, he snatched the microphone and joined her on the stage.

"If I could just steal your attention for a moment, ladies and gentlemen," David's voice filled the room. His mischief was gone; pride shone in his eyes.

Monique's heart jackhammered. What is he doing? She tried to pull the mic back, cheeks hot with embarrassment, but he held it.

"Tonight," he announced, sweeping his gaze across the crowd, "you were lucky enough to hear Monique Chambers—the best damn singer in this city, and soon, the best damn singer on the entire Pacific Ocean!"

The crowd roared. Monique stared at him, stunned.

He continued. "This isn't just her last gig at Sips and Stories. This is Monique's last night performing at a venue in Brisbane, period!"

He grabbed her hand and held it aloft. "She's off to chase her dreams as a singer aboard the Pacific Sun, and she is never looking back. Let's give her the send-off she deserves!"

The last of Monique's internal walls softened.

Sammie and Maggie emerged from the crowd and joined them on stage. She squeezed them both and whispered, "Thank you. For everything."

She turned to David. He grinned, pleased with his theatrics. She jabbed his arm playfully. "You're going to regret that public announcement, David Sparks."

"Doubtful, plus I'm sure I can handle whatever punishment you had in mind," he winked before folding her into a quick, claiming kiss.

The room thrummed with celebration. As the crowd began to thin. Monique retrieved the sleek silver camera Kyle and Cara had given her and took a quick picture of Sammy and Maggie behind the bar. When she looked up, David was already reaching for her hand.

They stepped out into the cool Brisbane night, fingers intertwined. She looked across at his stupidly handsome face and relished the warmth of his palm. *I Love you.* She thought. *I love you, I love you, I love you.*

For a second, the urge to fix everything—say the three words she'd kept folded inside her—rose so fierce she could taste it. Saying "I love you" tonight would mean leaving a rupture she couldn't undo. So she tucked the words back, pressed his hand, and let the silence stand between them like a promise and a warning all at once.

Chapter 36

Monique

Monique stood at the edge of the dock on a blistering hot December day, her suitcase beside her, the looming white cruise ship casting a long shadow across the pavement. The breeze tugged at her thick waves, and she clutched her boarding pass like it was the last tether to the life she was leaving behind.

This was it. The moment her life would change forever. There was no going back now.

David hadn't said much on the drive over. Just the usual banter, the kind that masked something deeper. She paid too close attention to the lyrics of **"Amazing" by Alex Lloyd** on the radio, letting them fill the silence he wouldn't.

She figured he was trying to keep the mood light—trying not to make this harder than it already was.

But she couldn't stop thinking about how amazing they were together, and how the dream she was finally realising would unravel all of it.

They'd never have that again.

This was the end. Of them.

She would be alone again, adrift in a sea of strangers.

But this is what she wanted. Wasn't it?

David stood beside her, quieter than she'd imagined, his presence steady, almost serene. She'd braced for an outburst—*Please stay with me, Don't go,*

I need you here. Something raw. Something desperate. Because he loved her... didn't he? And a man in love wouldn't just let her walk away.

But no. He didn't beg. And maybe that was the hardest part.

She told herself this was what she wanted. Had *always* wanted. This dream—this ship, this escape—had been her ultimate goal long before David ever entered the picture. And yet, since he did, everything had shifted, and she began to question everything except for the love she had for him.

"Well," she said tentatively, trying to keep her voice steady, "I guess this is goodbye."

David didn't flinch. His gaze held hers, calm and unreadable.

"I get why you'd think that... but no. This isn't goodbye."

A pause. Just long enough for her breath to catch.

She blinked. "What do you mean?"

He hesitated—just a flicker—but it was enough to make her stomach twist. "I'm coming with you."

Her laugh came out too loud, too quick. "Like a stowaway? Very funny."

"I'm serious."

His expression was steady. No grin. No sarcasm. Just truth.

"Okay, explain yourself. Did you buy a boarding pass or something?"

"No. Even better."

He reached into his jacket pocket and pulled out a card—Paradise Cruises printed across the back. Identical to hers.

"I don't understand."

"Take a look."

He handed it to her. Her fingers trembled as she turned it over. His photo. His name. And in bold capital letters: EMPLOYEE. At the bottom: Bar Manager.

Monique stared at it; her breath caught somewhere between disbelief and joy. "Are you serious?"

"Dead serious."

She launched herself into his arms, squeezing him so tightly she felt his heartbeat sync with hers.

"I don't understand. How did you do this?"

"Sammy encouraged me to reach out to Larry. Asked if there were any openings. They had a bar manager position to fill; my qualification helped me secure it."

"That's why you were working so hard to finish your studies…"

He nodded. "I wanted to be ready. For this. For you."

"But what about Sips and Stories?"

"Dad and Maggie have it covered. Honestly, I was just an extra cog in their well-oiled machine. I've drained enough from my father—it's time to cut the tether and do something for myself. This is what I want. And I want to do it with you."

Monique's chest tightened. She hadn't prepared for this. She'd spent weeks bracing for the ache of leaving him behind. She'd finally allowed herself to love him fully—quietly, privately—knowing it would end in heartbreak. And now, just as she was ready to mourn him, he was here. Choosing her.

Her eyes welled. "David… I love you."

Those three life-altering words spilled out, raw and trembling.

He smiled, eyes soft. "I know. I love you too."

Kyle cleared his throat behind them, grinning like a proud older brother. "About bloody time."

David chuckled and reached into his satchel, pulling out a familiar black box. "Which reminds me…"

Monique gasped. "Is that—?"

"The same video camera your mum used for your home videos." David smiled, "I found it in storage. Figured it was time to start making new memories."

He turned to Kyle. "Mate, would you do the honours?"

Kyle took the camera, adjusting the viewfinder with practised ease. "You got it."

David ran back to Monique and stood beside her, both of them framed by the cruise ship behind them. Kyle hit record.

"We're here," David said, voice bright, "about to board the Pacific Sun for our first day working with Paradise Cruises. How are you feeling, Monique?"

She looked at him, then at the ship, then back at the camera. Her heart was full. Her future was calling. And for the first time, she wasn't walking into it alone.

"I'm happy," she said, voice thick with emotion. "This is everything I've ever wanted... and more."

Kyle lowered the camera, smiling. "You're gonna be great, both of you."

And as they turned toward the gangway, hand in hand, Monique knew this wasn't just the start of her dream. It was the start of theirs.

Epilogue

David

The sun was setting below the waves, casting molten gold and burnt orange across the rippling sea. The ship's deck glowed in the light, a floating world suspended between sky and water. Behind the bar, David slid a Vodka Sunrise across the counter—cherry perched, umbrella tilted just so.

"For the lady," he said with a grin.

She flashed him a wink and a cheeky smile. "Thank you, handsome."

David chuckled. "Anytime, Margaret. Enjoy."

She took a sip, adjusted her oversized sunglasses, and gave him a nod of approval. Sequins shimmered across her kaftan as she turned to leave, her silver curls catching the light.

Eighty-two, retired, and living her best life on the high seas.

David watched her go, still smiling. If she were a few decades younger in another life, a wink like that from her might've led to a one-night stand and a morning full of regrets. But that life was well and truly in the past now. Now he was addicted to the rhythm of ship life and to one woman. Monique.

A soft hush fell over the room as the lights dimmed and the band began to play. The piano struck its first chord, followed by the low hum of the bass and the gentle tap of brushes on a snare. Then came the voice.

"Ladies and gentlemen," Monique purred through the mic, her tone velvet-smooth, "let the evening wrap around you like silk. These melodies aren't just notes—they're whispers, sighs, and slow dances for your soul. If you feel a delicious tingle in your ear, don't be alarmed. That's just the sound of surrender. Let it in. Let it linger."

And then she sang **"You're Still the One" by Shania Twain**.

The room stilled. Forks paused mid-air. Conversations faded. Heads turned. Because when Monique sang, the world listened. Her voice didn't just fill the space—it transformed it. David had seen it happen night after night, and still, it hit him like the first time.

Nearly two years ago, he'd fallen for that voice. And the woman behind it. He'd followed her onto this ship, into this life, and never looked back.

He leaned against the bar, watching her. She wore a deep emerald gown that shimmered with every breath, her curls pinned high, her eyes closed as she lost herself in the music. She was radiant. Unstoppable.

And she was his.

If someone had told him back in 1999 that this would be his life—working on a cruise ship, travelling to exotic places, sharing a cabin and a dream with the love of his life—he would've laughed. Or cried. Or both. Because the version of himself back then didn't believe he deserved joy like this. Not after the void his mother left behind. That pain had carved something deep into him, something that told him he wasn't enough.

But he was wrong.

He'd found his place. Not in spite of who he was, but because of it. And Monique—Monique had seen him, all of him, and despite all his missteps and misgivings, she let him in and kept him.

As the final note of her song lingered in the air, Monique opened her eyes and found him across the room. Their gaze locked. She smiled—not the stage smile, but the real one. The one that said, *I see you. I'm still choosing you.*

Monique

Later that night, after the crowd had thinned and the stars had taken their place above the sea, Monique stood at the edge of the deck with David's arms wrapped around her. The ocean stretched endlessly before them, a velvet expanse kissed by moonlight. The ship hummed beneath their feet, steady and alive, like a heartbeat carrying them forward.

She leaned into him, her cheek resting against his chest, and whispered, "This still feels like a dream."

David kissed her temple. "Then let's never wake up."

She smiled, but her heart tugged with something deeper. Something older. Catherine.

Her mother's plans of travelling the world with her daughter by her side were never realised.

They used to sit on the couch watching Getaway with Catriona Rowntree on TV, imagining the places they'd go. Catherine would point to the screen and say, *"That's where we'll sip cocktails, darling, without a care in the world."* But cancer had stolen that dream before it could take shape. Monique had boarded this ship with Catherine in her heart, every step a tribute to the woman who raised her to be bold, to be independent, to never let a man define her.

And yet... here she was. Defined not by dependence, but by love. Real love. The kind that held her without clipping her wings. The kind Catherine never quite trusted, but Monique believed—deep down—her mother would have understood. Maybe even approved of.

Monique pictured her mother standing next to them on the deck, looking out across the ocean. A content smile spread across her face, and brown waves dancing in the breeze wearing her favourite hibiscus sundress.

Then she looked across at David. Carefree. Confident. Charming.

You'd like him, Mum, she thought. *He's a rascal, but you'd warm to him and love him as much as I do.*

She glanced at David, his eyes closed, his breath slow and content. He had followed her into this life—not to possess it, but to share it. To build something with her, not around her. And that mattered. That changed everything.

Monique let the silence stretch, the stars blinking above like distant blessings. She thought of the woman she used to be—the one who sang on street corners and treated commitment like a trap. The one who believed dreams were meant to be chased alone. That woman still lived inside her, but now she had someone beside her. Someone who didn't dim her light, but reflected it. Amplified it.

She reached for David's hand and gave it a gentle squeeze. He didn't speak. Just pressed a quiet kiss to her temple and held her closer.

The ship hummed beneath their feet, steady and alive, carrying them toward whatever came next. And with the future wide open ahead, they stayed there—two hearts, one horizon, and a love that had finally found its home.

Thank You

Thanks for choosing to read Y2K Betrayal. I am truly honoured that you took a chance on my novel, which is why this section is dedicated to you. As an indie author, I rely on word of mouth and reader support. So if you enjoyed the story, it would mean the world to me if you could leave a review for this book on **Amazon** and/or **Goodreads**. Every review counts towards someone else discovering this story.

Want to be the first to find out about upcoming releases, giveaways, ARC opportunities and get exclusive behind-the-scenes insights and updates on my stories?

Subscribe to my newsletter
www.taniaweatherley.com

Acknowledgements

I need to say a big thank you to Llianne Olivo and Rachel Hanly, two of my loudest supporters of Y2K Love and now beta readers for Y2K Betrayal, along with my new beta readers Rachael Dent and David Uptin. Your encouragement and support push me to keep writing. I also need to say thank you to my parents and husband, who have been taking care of me and my boys while recovering from my knee injury and surgery. My immobility may have thrown our family routine out of whack, but it also gave me the downtime to finish this book. I am recovering, and this book exists now thanks to them and their unwavering love.

About the Author

Tania is a Brisbane-based author with a love for writing authentic stories that are sweet and deep with a dash of heat. When she's not writing about characters falling in love and discovering self-love, she's a full-time mum to two energetic boys and a part-time marketer and content writer.

A lifelong fan of 90s/00s nostalgia, musicals, and stories in all forms (books, TV and movies), Tania also finds joy in exploring new places with her family, listening to audiobooks that make housework bearable, cozy gaming sessions, and the delightfully messy world of junk journaling and collage.

Also by Tania Weatherley

Schoolies '99

Love the nostalgia of the late 90s? Think every unforgettable moment deserves a soundtrack? *Then dive into* Schoolies '99—a coming-of-age Aussie prequel to Y2K Love. This novella drops you into the chaotic heart of Australia's iconic post-high school rite of passage, where friendship, holiday crushes and hard-won independence collide.

Y2K Love

If you long for the nostalgia of the late 90s and early 00s and believe every good story needs a soundtrack, you'll devour Y2K Love. This coming-of-age Aussie rom-com, set in the year 2000, weaves iconic songs of the era through a story that follows two best friends, Sarah and Lauren, as they navigate life and love during their first year of university in Australia.

www.ingramcontent.com/pod-product-compliance
Lightning Source LLC
Chambersburg PA
CBHW031236210726
48287CB00003B/790